TENNESSEE WILLIAMS

has won two Pulitzer Prizes and three New York Critics' Circle Awards—including one for THE NIGHT OF THE IGUANA.

This drama about human loneliness and man's yearning need for love has been hailed by the critics as one of the greatest plays of America's most important playwright.

"There it is. Destruction and creation, cruelty and compassion, smut and spirituality, all of the paradoxical ingredients so essential to the divine equation Mr. Williams uses to transform energy into living stage matter. And again he does so with the same style, humor, and sensitivity that make him the foremost American playwright of his time."

—Henry Hewes,
The Saturday Review

"Tennessee Williams is writing at the top of his form."
—Howard Taubman,
N. Y. Times

"A great Williams play"

—John McClain,
N. Y. Journal-American

"Williams is at his poetic, moving best with Night of the Iguana. . . . It will haunt you; haunt you with things said and unsaid; haunt you with its beauty . . . Williams has given us one of his finest dramas."

—John Chapman,
N. Y. Daily News

This Signet edition includes eight pages of scenes from the sensational new film starring Richard Burton, Ava Gardner, Deborah Kerr, Sue Lyons.

By TENNESSEE WILLIAMS

PLAYS

The Glass Menagerie
27 Wagons Full of Cotton and Other Plays
A Streetcar Named Desire *
Summer and Smoke
The Rose Tattoo
Camino Real
You Touched Me (with Donald Windham)
Orpheus Descending (and Battle of Angels)
(Signet title: The Fugitive Kind)
Baby Doll (a screenplay)
Suddenly Last Summer *
Cat on a Hot Tin Roof *
Sweet Bird of Youth *
Period of Adjustment
The Milk Train Doesn't Stop Here Any More
The Seven Descents of Myrtle

POETRY

Five Young American Poets, 1944
In the Winter of Cities

PROSE

The Roman Spring of Mrs. Stone
One Arm and Other Stories
Hard Candy and Other Stories

* Titles available in SIGNET editions

TENNESSEE WILLIAMS

The Night of the Iguana

And so, as kinsmen met a night,
We talked between the rooms,
Until the moss had reached our lips,
And covered up our names.
EMILY DICKINSON

A SIGNET BOOK from
NEW AMERICAN LIBRARY
TIMES MIRROR

The epigraph by Emily Dickinson is from *The Poems of Emily
Dickinson,* published by Little, Brown & Co.

*This is an authorized reprint of a hardcover edition published
by New Directions.*

SEVENTH PRINTING

SIGNET TRADEMARK REG. U.S. PAT. OFF. AND FOREIGN COUNTRIES
REGISTERED TRADEMARK—MARCA REGISTRADA
HECHO EN CHICAGO, U.S.A.

SIGNET, SIGNET CLASSICS, SIGNETTE, MENTOR AND PLUME BOOKS
*are published by The New American Library, Inc.,
1301 Avenue of the Americas, New York, New York 10019*

PRINTED IN THE UNITED STATES OF AMERICA

The play takes place in the summer of 1940 in a rather rustic and very Bohemian hotel, the Costa Verde, which, as its name implies, sits on a jungle-covered hilltop overlooking the "caleta," or "morning beach" of Puerto Barrio in Mexico. But this is decidedly not the Puerto Barrio of today. At that time—twenty years ago—the west coast of Mexico had not yet become the Las Vegas and Miami Beach of Mexico. The villages were still predominantly primitive Indian villages, and the still-water morning beach of Puerto Barrio and the rain forests above it were among the world's wildest and loveliest populated places.

The setting for the play is the wide verandah of the hotel. This roofed verandah, enclosed by a railing, runs around all four sides of the somewhat dilapidated, tropical-style frame structure, but on the stage we see only the front and one side. Below the verandah, which is slightly raised above the stage level, are shrubs with vivid trumpet-shaped flowers and a few cactus plants, while at the sides we see the foliage of the encroaching jungle. A tall coconut palm slants upward at one side, its trunk notched for a climber to chop down coconuts for rum-cocos. In the back wall of the verandah are the doors of a line of small cubicle bedrooms which are screened with mosquito-net curtains. For the night scenes they are lighted from within, so that each cubicle appears as a little interior stage, the curtains giving a misty effect to their dim inside lighting. A path which goes down through the rain forest to the highway and the beach, its opening masked by foliage, leads off from one side of the verandah. A canvas hammock is strung from posts on the verandah and there are a few old wicker rockers and rattan lounging chairs at one side.

The Night of the Iguana was presented at the Royale Theatre in New York on December 28, 1961 by Charles Bowden, in association with Violla Rubber. It was directed by Frank Corsaro; the stage setting was designed by Oliver Smith; lighting by Jean Rosenthal; costumes by Noel Taylor; audio effects by Edward Beyer. The cast, in order of appearance, was as follows:

MAXINE FAULK	BETTE DAVIS
PEDRO	JAMES FARENTINO
PANCHO	CHRISTOPHER JONES
REVEREND SHANNON	PATRICK O'NEAL
HANK	THESEUS GEORGE
HERR FAHRENKOPF	HEINZ HOHENWALD
FRAU FAHRENKOPF	LUCY LANDAU
WOLFGANG	BRUCE GLOVER
HILDA	LARYSSA LAURET
JUDITH FELLOWES	PATRICIA ROE
HANNAH JELKES	MARGARET LEIGHTON
CHARLOTTE GOODALL	LANE BRADBURY
JONATHAN COFFIN (NONNO)	ALAN WEBB
JAKE LATTA	LOUIS GUSS

Production owned and presented by "The Night of the Iguana" Joint Venture (the joint venture consisting of Charles Bowden and Two Rivers Enterprises, Inc.).

Act One

As the curtain rises, there are sounds of a party of excited female tourists arriving by bus on the road down the hill below the Costa Verde Hotel. MRS. MAXINE FAULK, *the proprietor of the hotel, comes around the turn of the verandah. She is a stout, swarthy woman in her middle forties—affable and rapaciously lusty. She is wearing a pair of levis and a blouse that is half unbuttoned. She is followed by* PEDRO, *a Mexican of about twenty—slim and attractive. He is an employee in the hotel and also her casual lover.* PEDRO *is stuffing his shirt under the belt of his pants and sweating as if he had been working hard in the sun.* MRS. FAULK *looks down the hill and is pleased by the sight of someone coming up from the tourist bus below.*

MAXINE [*calling out*]: Shannon! [*A man's voice from below answers:* "Hi!"] Hah! [MAXINE *always laughs with a single harsh, loud bark, opening her mouth like a seal expecting a fish to be thrown to it.*] My spies told me that you were back under the border! [*to* PEDRO] Anda, hombre, anda!

[MAXINE'S *delight expands and vibrates in her as* SHANNON *labors up the hill to the hotel. He does not appear on the jungle path for a minute or two after the shouting between them starts.*]

MAXINE: Hah! My spies told me you went through Saltillo last week with a busload of women—a whole busload of females, all females, hah! How many you laid so far? Hah!

SHANNON [*from below, panting*]: Great Caesar's ghost . . . stop . . . shouting!

MAXINE: No wonder your ass is draggin', hah!

9

SHANNON: Tell the kid to help me up with this bag.

MAXINE [*shouting directions*]: Pedro! Anda—la maleta. Pancho, no seas flojo! Va y trae el equipaje del señor.

[PANCHO, *another young Mexican, comes around the verandah and trots down the jungle path.* PEDRO *has climbed up a coconut tree with a machete and is chopping down nuts for rum-cocos.*]

SHANNON [*shouting, below*]: Fred? Hey, Fred!

MAXINE [*with a momentary gravity*]: Fred can't hear you, Shannon. [*She goes over and picks up a coconut, shaking it against her ear to see if it has milk in it.*]

SHANNON [*still below*]: Where is Fred—gone fishing?

[MAXINE *lops the end off a coconut with the machete, as* PANCHO *trots up to the verandah with* SHANNON'S *bag—a beat-up Gladstone covered with travel stickers from all over the world. Then* SHANNON *appears, in a crumpled white linen suit. He is panting, sweating and wild-eyed. About thirty-five,* SHANNON *is "black Irish." His nervous state is terribly apparent; he is a young man who has cracked up before and is going to crack up again—perhaps repeatedly.*]

MAXINE: Well! Lemme look at you!

SHANNON: Don't look at me, get dressed!

MAXINE: Gee, you look like you had it!

SHANNON: You look like you been having it, too. Get dressed!

MAXINE: Hell, I'm dressed. I never dress in September. Don't you know I never dress in September?

SHANNON: Well, just, just—button your shirt up.

MAXINE: How long you been off it, Shannon?

SHANNON: Off what?

MAXINE: The wagon . . .

SHANNON: Hell, I'm dizzy with fever. Hundred and three this morning in Cuernavaca.

MAXINE: Watcha got wrong with you?

SHANNON: Fever . . . fever . . . Where's Fred?

MAXINE: Dead.

SHANNON: Did you say *dead?*

MAXINE: That's what I said. Fred is dead.

SHANNON: How?

MAXINE: Less'n two weeks ago, Fred cut his hand on a fish-hook, it got infected, infection got in his blood stream, and he was dead inside of forty-eight hours. [*to* PANCHO] Vete!

SHANNON: Holy smoke. . . .

MAXINE: I can't quite realize it yet. . . .

SHANNON: You don't seem—inconsolable about it.

MAXINE: Fred was an old man, baby. Ten years older'n me. We hadn't had sex together in. . . .

SHANNON: What's that got to do with it?

MAXINE: Lie down and have a rum-coco.

SHANNON: No, no. I want a cold beer. If I start drinking rum-cocos now I won't stop drinking rum-cocos. So Fred is dead? I looked forward to lying in this hammock and talking to Fred.

MAXINE: Well Fred's not talking now, Shannon. A diabetic

gets a blood infection, he goes like that without a decent hospital in less'n a week. [*A bus horn is heard blowing from below.*] Why don't your busload of women come on up here? They're blowing the bus horn down there.

SHANNON: Let 'em blow it, blow it. . . . [*He sways a little.*] I got a fever. [*He goes to the top of the path, divides the flowering bushes and shouts down the hill to the bus.*] Hank! Hank! Get them out of the bus and bring 'em up here! Tell 'em the rates are OK. Tell 'em the. . . . [*His voice gives out, and he stumbles back to the verandah, where he sinks down onto the low steps, panting.*] Absolutely the worst party I've ever been out with in ten years of conducting tours. For God's sake, help me with 'em because I can't go on. I got to rest here a while. [*She gives him a cold beer.*] Thanks. Look and see if they're getting out of the bus. [*She crosses to the masking foliage and separates it to look down the hill.*] Are they getting out of the bus or are they staying in it, the stingy—daughters of—bitches. . . . Schoolteachers at a Baptist Female College in Blowing Rock, Texas. Eleven, eleven of them.

MAXINE: A football squad of old maids.

SHANNON: Yeah, and I'm the football. Are they out of the bus?

MAXINE: One's gotten out—she's going into the bushes.

SHANNON: Well, I've got the ignition key to the bus in my pocket—this pocket—so they can't continue without me unless they walk.

MAXINE: They're still blowin' that horn.

SHANNON: Fantastic. I can't lose this party. Blake Tours has put me on probation because I had a bad party last month that tried to get me sacked and I am now on probation with Blake Tours. If I lose this party I'll be sacked for sure . . . Ah, my God, are they still all in the bus? [*He heaves himself off the steps and staggers back to the path, dividing the foliage to look down it, then shouts.*] Hank! Get them out of the busssss! Bring them up heeee-re!

HANK'S VOICE [*from below*]: They wanta go back in tooooooowwww-n.

SHANNON: They *can't* go back in tooooowwwwn!—Whew—Five years ago this summer I was conducting round-the-world tours for Cook's. Exclusive groups of retired Wall Street financiers. We traveled in fleets of Pierce Arrows and Hispano Suizas.—Are they getting out of the bus?

MAXINE: You're going to pieces, are you?

SHANNON: No! Gone! Gone! [*He rises and shouts down the hill again.*] Hank! come up here! Come on up here a minute! I wanta talk to you about this situation!—Incredible, fantastic . . . [*He drops back on the steps, his head falling into his hands.*]

MAXINE: They're not getting out of the bus.—Shannon . . . you're not in a nervous condition to cope with this party, Shannon, so let them go and you stay.

SHANNON: You know my situation: I lose this job, what's next? There's nothing lower than Blake Tours, Maxine honey. —Are they getting out of the bus? Are they getting out of it now?

MAXINE: Man's comin' up the hill.

SHANNON: Aw. Hank. You gotta help me with him.

MAXINE: I'll give him a rum-coco.

[HANK *comes grinning onto the verandah.*]

HANK: Shannon, them ladies are not gonna come up here, so you better come on back to the bus.

SHANNON: Fantastic.—I'm not going down to the bus and I've got the ignition key to the bus in my pocket. It's going to stay in my pocket for the next three days.

HANK: You can't get away with that, Shannon. Hell, they'll walk back to town if you don't give up the bus key.

SHANNON: They'd drop like flies from sunstrokes on that road. . . . Fantastic, absolutely fantastic . . . [*Panting and sweating, he drops a hand on* HANK's *shoulder.*] Hank, I want your co-operation. Can I have it? Because when you're out with a difficult party like this, the tour conductor—me—and the guide—you—have got to stick together to control the situations as they come up against us. It's a test of strength between two men, in this case, and a busload of old wet *hens!* You know that, don't you?

HANK: Well. . . . [*He chuckles.*] There's this kid that's crying on the back seat all the time, and that's what's rucked up the deal. Hell, I don't know if you did or you didn't, but they all think that you did 'cause the kid keeps crying.

SHANNON: *Hank? Look!* I don't care what they think. A tour conducted by T. Lawrence Shannon is in his charge, completely—where to go, when to go, every detail of it. Otherwise I resign. So go on back down there and get them out of that bus before they suffocate in it. Haul them out by force if necessary and herd them up here. Hear me? Don't give me any argument about it. Mrs. Faulk, honey? Give him a menu, give him one of your sample menus to show the ladies. She's got a Chinaman cook here, you won't believe the menu. The cook's from Shanghai, handled the kitchen at an exclusive club there. I got him here for her, and he's a bug, a fanatic about— whew!—continental cuisine . . . can even make beef Stroganoff and thermidor dishes. Mrs. Faulk, honey? Hand him one of those—whew!—one of those fantastic sample menus. [MAXINE *chuckles, as if perpetrating a practical joke, as she hands him a sheet of paper.*] Thanks. Now, here. Go on back down there and show them this fantastic menu. Describe the view from the hill, and . . . [HANK *accepts the menu with a chuckling shake of the head.*] And have a cold Carta Blanca and. . . .

HANK: You better go down with me.

SHANNON: I can't leave this verandah for at least forty-eight hours. *What in blazes is this?* A little animated cartoon by Hieronymus Bosch?

[*The German family which is staying at the hotel, the* FAHRENKOPFS, *their daughter and son-in-law, suddenly make a startling, dreamlike entrance upon the scene. They troop around the verandah, then turn down into the jungle path. They are all dressed in the minimal concession to decency and all are pink and gold like baroque cupids in various sizes—Rubenesque, splendidly physical. The bride,* HILDA, *walks astride a big inflated rubber horse which has an ecstatic smile and great winking eyes. She shouts "Horsey, horsey, giddap!" as she waddles astride it, followed by her Wagnerian-tenor bridegroom,* WOLFGANG, *and her father,* HERR FAHRENKOPF, *a tank manufacturer from Frankfurt. He is carrying a portable shortwave radio, which is tuned in to the crackle and guttural voices of a German broadcast reporting the Battle of Britain.* FRAU FAHRENKOPF, *bursting with rich, healthy fat and carrying a basket of food for a picnic at the beach, brings up the rear. They begin to sing a Nazi marching song.*]

SHANNON: Aw—Nazis. How come there's so many of them down here lately?

MAXINE: Mexico's the front door to South America—and the back door to the States, that's why.

SHANNON: Aw, and you're setting yourself up here as a receptionist at both doors, now that Fred's dead? [MAXINE *comes over and sits down on him in the hammock.*] Get off my pelvis before you crack it. If you want to crack something, crack some ice for my forehead. [*She removes a chunk of ice from her glass and massages his forehead with it.*]—Ah, God. . . .

MAXINE [*chuckling*]: Ha, so you took the young chick and the old hens are squawking about it, Shannon?

SHANNON: The kid asked for it, no kidding, but she's seventeen—less, a month less'n seventeen. So it's serious, it's very serious, because the kid is not just emotionally precocious, she's a musical prodigy, too.

MAXINE: What's that got to do with it?

SHANNON: Here's what it's got to do with it, she's traveling under the wing, the military escort, of this, this—butch vocal teacher who organizes little community sings in the bus. Ah, God! I'm surprised they're not singing now, they must've already suffocated. Or they'd be singing some morale-boosting number like "She's a Jolly Good Fellow" or "Pop Goes the Weasel."—Oh, God. . . . [MAXINE *chuckles up and down the scale.*] And each night after supper, after the complaints about the supper and the check-up on the checks by the math instructor, and the vomiting of the supper by several ladies, who have inspected the kitchen—then the kid, the canary, will give a vocal recital. She opens her mouth and out flies Carrie Jacobs Bond or Ethelbert Nevin. I mean after a day of one indescribable torment after another, such as three blowouts, and a leaking radiator in Tierra Caliente. . . . [*He sits up slowly in the hammock as these recollections gather force.*] And an evening climb up sierras, through torrents of rain, around hairpin turns over gorges and chasms measureless to man, and with a Thermos-jug under the driver's seat which the Baptist College ladies think is filled with icewater but which I know is filled with iced tequila—I mean after such a day has finally come to a close, the musical prodigy, Miss Charlotte Goodall, right after supper, before there's a chance to escape, will give a heartbreaking and earsplitting rendition of Carrie Jacobs Bond's "End of a Perfect Day"—with absolutely no humor. . . .

MAXINE: Hah!

SHANNON: Yeah, "Hah!" Last night—no, night before last, the bus burned out its brake linings in Chilpancingo. This town has a hotel . . . this hotel has a piano, which hasn't been tuned since they shot Maximilian. This Texas songbird opens her mouth and out flies "I Love You Truly," and it flies straight at *me,* with *gestures,* all right at *me,* till her chaperone, this Diesel-driven vocal instructor of hers, slams the piano lid down and hauls her out of the mess hall. But as she's hauled out Miss Bird-Girl opens her mouth and out flies, "Larry, Larry, I love you, I love you truly!" That night, when I went to my room, I found that I had a roommate.

MAXINE: The musical prodigy had moved in with you?

SHANNON: The *spook* had moved in with me. In that hot room with one bed, the width of an ironing board and about as hard, the spook was up there on it, sweating, stinking, grinning up at me.

MAXINE: Aw, the spook. [*She chuckles.*] So you've got the spook with you again.

SHANNON: That's right, he's the only passenger that got off the bus with me, honey.

MAXINE: Is he here now?

SHANNON: Not far.

MAXINE: On the verandah?

SHANNON: He might be on the other side of the verandah. Oh, he's around somewhere, but he's like the Sioux Indians in the Wild West fiction, he doesn't attack before sundown, he's an after-sundown shadow. . . .

[SHANNON *wriggles out of the hammock as the bus horn gives one last, long protesting blast.*]

MAXINE:

> I have a little shadow
> That goes in and out with me,
> And what can be the use of him
> Is more than I can see.
>
> He's very, very like me,
> From his heels up to his head,
> And he always hops before me
> When I hop into my bed.

SHANNON: That's the truth. He sure hops in the bed with me.

MAXINE: When you're sleeping alone, or . . . ?

SHANNON: I haven't slept in three nights.

MAXINE: Aw, you will tonight, baby.

[*The bus horn sounds again.* SHANNON *rises and squints down the hill at the bus.*]

SHANNON: How long's it take to sweat the faculty of a Baptist Female College out of a bus that's parked in the sun when it's a hundred degrees in the shade?

MAXINE: They're staggering out of it now.

SHANNON: Yeah, I've won *this* round, I reckon. What're they doing down there, can you see?

MAXINE: They're crowding around your pal Hank.

SHANNON: Tearing him to pieces?

MAXINE: One of them's slapped him, he's ducked back into the bus, and she is starting up here.

SHANNON: Oh, Great Caesar's ghost, it's the butch vocal teacher.

MISS FELLOWES [*in a strident voice, from below*]: Shannon! Shannon!

SHANNON: For God's sake, help me with her.

MAXINE: You know I'll help you, baby, but why don't you lay off the young ones and cultivate an interest in normal grown-up women?

MISS FELLOWES [*her voice coming nearer*]: Shannon!

SHANNON [*shouting down the hill*]: Come on up, Miss Fellowes, everything's fixed. [*to* MAXINE] Oh, God, here she comes chargin' up the hill like a bull elephant on a rampage!

[MISS FELLOWES *thrashes through the foliage at the top of the jungle path.*]

SHANNON: Miss Fellowes, never do that! Not at high noon in a tropical country in summer. Never charge up a hill like you were leading a troop of cavalry attacking an almost impregnable. . . .

MISS FELLOWES [*panting and furious*]: I don't want advice or instructions, I want the *bus key!*

SHANNON: Mrs. Faulk, this is Miss Judith Fellowes.

MISS FELLOWES: Is this man making a deal with you?

MAXINE: I don't know what you—

MISS FELLOWES: Is this man getting a *kickback* out of you?

MAXINE: Nobody gets any kickback out of me. I turn away more people than—

MISS FELLOWES [*cutting in*]: This isn't the Ambos Mundos. It says in the brochure that in Puerto Barrio we stay at the Ambos Mundos in the heart of the city.

SHANNON: Yes, on the plaza—tell her about the plaza.

MAXINE: What about the plaza?

SHANNON: It's hot, noisy, stinking, swarming with flies. Pariah dogs dying in the—

MISS FELLOWES: How is this place better?

SHANNON: The view from this verandah is equal and I think better than the view from Victoria Peak in Hong Kong, the view from the roof-terrace of the Sultan's palace in—

MISS FELLOWES [*cutting in*]: I want the view of a clean bed, a bathroom with plumbing that works, and food that is eatable and digestible and not contaminated by filthy—

SHANNON: *Miss Fellowes!*

MISS FELLOWES: Take your hand off my arm.

SHANNON: Look at this sample menu. The cook is a Chinese imported from Shanghai by *me!* Sent here by *me*, year before last, in nineteen thirty-eight. He was the chef at the Royal Colonial Club in—

MISS FELLOWES [*cutting in*]: You got a telephone here?

MAXINE: Sure, in the office.

MISS FELLOWES: I want to use it— I'll call collect. Where's the office?

MAXINE [*to* PANCHO]: Llévala al teléfono!

[*With* PANCHO *showing her the way,* MISS FELLOWES *stalks off around the verandah to the office.* SHANNON *falls back, sighing desperately, against the verandah wall.*]

MAXINE: Hah!

SHANNON: Why did you have to . . . ?

MAXINE: Huh?

SHANNON: Come out looking like this! For you it's funny but for me it's. . . .

MAXINE: This is how I *look*. What's wrong with how I *look?*

SHANNON: I told you to button your shirt. Are you so proud of your boobs that you won't button your shirt up?—Go in the office and see if she's calling Blake Tours to get me fired.

MAXINE: She better not unless she pays for the call.

[*She goes around the turn of the verandah.*]

[MISS HANNAH JELKES *appears below the verandah steps and*

stops short as SHANNON *turns to the wall, pounding his fist
against it with a sobbing sound in his throat.*]

HANNAH: Excuse me.

[SHANNON *looks down at her, dazed.* HANNAH *is remarkable-
looking—ethereal, almost ghostly. She suggests a Gothic
cathedral image of a medieval saint, but animated. She could
be thirty, she could be forty: she is totally feminine and yet
androgynous-looking—almost timeless. She is wearing a cotton print dress and has a bag slung on a strap over her
shoulder.*]

HANNAH: Is this the Costa Verde Hotel?

SHANNON [*suddenly pacified by her appearance*]: Yes. Yes,
it is.

HANNAH: Are you . . . you're not, the hotel manager, are
you?

SHANNON: No. She'll be right back.

HANNAH: Thank you. Do you have any idea if they have two
vacancies here? One for myself and one for my grandfather
who's waiting in a taxi down there on the road. I didn't want
to bring him up the hill—till I'd made sure they have rooms
for us first.

SHANNON: Well, there's plenty of room here out-of-season—
like now.

HANNAH: Good! Wonderful! I'll get him out of the taxi.

SHANNON: Need any help?

HANNAH: No, thank you. We'll make it all right.

[*She gives him a pleasant nod and goes back off down the
path through the rain forest. A coconut plops to the ground;
a parrot screams at a distance.* SHANNON *drops into the hammock and stretches out. Then* MAXINE *reappears.*]

SHANNON: How about the call? Did she make a phone call?

MAXINE: She called a judge in Texas—Blowing Rock, Texas. Collect.

SHANNON: She's trying to get me fired and she is also trying to pin on me a rape charge, a charge of statutory rape.

MAXINE: What's "statutory rape"? I've never known what that was.

SHANNON: That's when a man is seduced by a girl under twenty. [*She chuckles.*] It's not funny, Maxine honey.

MAXINE: Why do you want the young ones—or think that you do?

SHANNON: I don't want any, any—regardless of age.

MAXINE: Then why do you take them, Shannon? [*He swallows but does not answer.*]—Huh, Shannon.

SHANNON: People need human contact, Maxine honey.

MAXINE: What size shoe do you wear?

SHANNON: I don't get the point of that question.

MAXINE: These shoes are shot and if I remember correctly, you travel with only one pair. Fred's estate included one good pair of shoes and your feet look about his size.

SHANNON: I loved ole Fred but I don't want to fill his shoes, honey.

[*She has removed* SHANNON'S *beat-up, English-made ox-fords.*]

MAXINE: Your socks are shot. Fred's socks would fit you, too, Shannon. [*She opens his collar.*] Aw-aw, I see you got on your gold cross. That's a bad sign, it means you're thinking again about goin' back to the Church.

SHANNON: This is my last tour, Maxine. I wrote my old Bishop this morning a complete confession and a complete capitulation.

[*She takes a letter from his damp shirt pocket.*]

MAXINE: If this is the letter, baby, you've sweated through it, so the old bugger couldn't read it even if you mailed it to him this time.

[*She has started around the verandah, and goes off as* HANK *reappears up the hill-path, mopping his face.* SHANNON'S *relaxed position in the hammock aggravates* HANK *sorely.*]

HANK: Will you get your ass out of that hammock?

SHANNON: No, I will not.

HANK: Shannon, git out of that hammock! [*He kicks at* SHANNON'S *hips in the hammock.*]

SHANNON: Hank, if you can't function under rough circumstances, you are in the wrong racket, man. I gave you instructions, the instructions were simple. I said get them out of the bus and. . . .

[MAXINE *comes back with a kettle of water, a towel and other shaving equipment.*]

HANK: Out of the hammock, Shannon! [*He kicks* SHANNON *again, harder.*]

SHANNON [*warningly*]: That's enough, Hank. A little familiarity goes a long way, but not as far as you're going. [MAXINE *starts lathering his face.*] What's this, what are you . . . ?

MAXINE: Haven't you ever had a shave-and-haircut by a lady barber?

HANK: The kid has gone into hysterics.

MAXINE: Hold still, Shannon.

SHANNON: Hank, hysteria is a natural phenomenon, the common denominator of the female nature. It's the big female weapon, and the test of a man is his ability to cope with it, and I can't believe you can't. If I believed that you couldn't, I would not be able—

MAXINE: Hold still!

SHANNON: I'm holding still. [*to* HANK] No, I wouldn't be able to take you out with me again. So go on back down there and—

HANK: You want me to go back down there and tell them you're getting a shave up here in a hammock?

MAXINE: Tell them that Reverend Larry is going back to the Church so they can go back to the Female College in Texas.

HANK: I want another beer.

MAXINE: Help yourself, piggly-wiggly, the cooler's in my office right around there. [*She points around the corner of the verandah.*]

SHANNON [*as* HANK *goes off*]: It's horrible how you got to bluff and keep bluffing even when hollering "Help!" is all you're up to, Maxine. *You cut me!*

MAXINE: You didn't hold still.

SHANNON: Just trim the beard a little.

MAXINE: I know. Baby, tonight we'll go night-swimming, whether it storms or not.

SHANNON: Ah, God. . . .

MAXINE: The Mexican kids are wonderful night-swimmers. . . . Hah, when I found 'em they were taking the two-hundred-foot dives off the Quebrada, but the Quebrada Hotel kicked 'em out for being over-attentive to the lady guests there. That's how I got hold of them.

SHANNON: Maxine, you're bigger than life and twice as unnatural, honey.

MAXINE: No one's bigger than life-size, Shannon, or even
ever that big, except maybe Fred. [*She shouts "Fred?" and
gets a faint answering echo from an adjoining hill.*] Little Sir
Echo is all that answers for him now, Shannon, but. . . . [*She
pats some bay rum on his face.*] Dear old Fred was always a
mystery to me. He was so patient and tolerant with me that it
was insulting to me. A man and a woman have got to challenge
each other, y'know what I mean. I mean I hired those diving-
boys from the Quebrada six months before Fred died, and did
he care? Did he give a damn when I started night-swimming
with them? No. He'd go night-*fishing*, all night, and when I
got up the next day, he'd be preparing to go out fishing again,
but he just caught the fish and threw them back in the sea.

[HANK *returns and sits drinking his beer on the steps.*]

SHANNON: The mystery of old Fred was simple. He was just
cool and decent, that's all the mystery of him. . . . Get your
pair of night-swimmers to grab my ladies' luggage out of the
bus before the vocal-teacher gets off the phone and stops them.

MAXINE [*shouting*]: Pedro! Pancho! Muchachos! Trae las
maletas al anejo! Pronto! [*The Mexican boys start down the
path.* MAXINE *sits in the hammock beside* SHANNON.] You I'll
put in Fred's old room, next to me.

SHANNON: You want me in his socks and his shoes and in
his room next to *you*? [*He stares at her with a shocked surmise of her intentions toward him, then flops back down in
the hammock with an incredulous laugh.*] Oh no, honey. I've
just been hanging on till I could get in this hammock on this
verandah over the rain forest and the still-water beach, that's
all that can pull me through this last tour in a condition to go
back to my . . . original . . . vocation.

MAXINE: Hah, you still have some rational moments when
you face the fact that churchgoers don't go to church to hear
atheistical sermons.

SHANNON: Goddamit, I never preached an atheistical sermon in a church in my life, and. . . .

[MISS FELLOWES *has charged out of the office and rounds the verandah to bear down on* SHANNON *and* MAXINE, *who jumps up out of the hammock.*]

MISS FELLOWES: I've completed my call, which I made collect to Texas.

[MAXINE *shrugs, going by her around the verandah.* MISS FELLOWES *runs across the verandah.*]

SHANNON [*sitting up in the hammock*]: Excuse me, Miss Fellowes, for not getting out of this hammock, but I . . . Miss Fellowes? Please sit down a minute, I want to confess something to you.

MISS FELLOWES: That ought to be int'restin'! *What?*

SHANNON: Just that—well, like everyone else, at some point or other in life, my life has cracked up on me.

MISS FELLOWES: How does that compensate *us?*

SHANNON: I don't think I know what you mean by *compensate*, Miss Fellowes. [*He props himself up and gazes at her with the gentlest bewilderment, calculated to melt a heart of stone.*] I mean I've just confessed to you that I'm at the end of my rope, and you say, "How does that compensate *us?*" Please, Miss Fellowes. Don't make me feel that any adult human being puts personal compensation before the dreadful, bare fact of a man at the end of his rope who still has to try to go on, to continue, as if he'd never been better or stronger in his whole existence. No, don't do that, it would. . . .

MISS FELLOWES: It would *what?*

SHANNON: Shake if not shatter everything left of my faith in essential . . . human . . . *goodness!*

MAXINE [*returning, with a pair of socks*]: Hah!

MISS FELLOWES: Can you sit there, I mean lie there—yeah, I mean *lie* there . . . ! and talk to me about—

MAXINE: Hah!

MISS FELLOWES: "Essential human goodness"? Why, just plain human decency is beyond your imagination, Shannon, so lie there, lie there and *lie* there, we're *going!*

SHANNON [*rising from the hammock*]: Miss Fellowes, I thought that I was conducting this party, not you.

MISS FELLOWES: You? You just now *admitted* you're incompetent, as well as. . . .

MAXINE: Hah.

SHANNON: Maxine, will you—

MISS FELLOWES [*cutting in with cold, righteous fury*]: Shannon, we girls have worked and slaved all year at Baptist Female College for this Mexican tour, and the tour is a cheat!

SHANNON [*to himself*]: Fantastic!

MISS FELLOWES: Yes, *cheat!* You haven't stuck to the schedule and you haven't stuck to the itinerary advertised in the brochure which Blake Tours put out. Now either Blake Tours is cheating us or you are cheating Blake Tours, and I'm putting wheels in motion—I don't care *what* it costs me —I'm. . . .

SHANNON: Oh, Miss Fellowes, isn't it just as plain to you as it is to me that your hysterical insults, which are not at all easy for any born and bred gentleman to accept, are not . . . *motivated, provoked* by . . . anything as *trivial* as the, the . . . the motivations that you're, you're . . . *ascribing* them to? Now can't we talk about the *real, true* cause of. . . .

MISS FELLOWES: Cause of *what?*

[CHARLOTTE GOODALL *appears at the top of the hill.*]

SHANNON: —Cause of your *rage* Miss Fellowes, your—

MISS FELLOWES: *Charlotte! Stay down the hill in the bus!*

CHARLOTTE: Judy, they're—

MISS FELLOWES: *Obey me! Down!*

[CHARLOTTE *retreats from view like a well-trained dog.* MISS FELLOWES *charges back to* SHANNON *who has gotten out of the hammock. He places a conciliatory hand on her arm.*]

MISS FELLOWES: *Take your hand off my arm!*

MAXINE: Hah!

SHANNON: *Fantastic.* Miss Fellowes, please! No more shouting? Please? Now I really must ask you to let this party of ladies come up here and judge the accommodations for themselves and compare them with what they saw passing through town. Miss Fellowes, there is such a thing as charm and beauty in some places, as much as there's nothing but dull, ugly imitation of highway motels in Texas and—

[MISS FELLOWES *charges over to the path to see if* CHARLOTTE *has obeyed her.* SHANNON *follows, still propitiatory.* MAXINE *says "Hah," but she gives him an affectionate little pat as he goes by her. He pushes her hand away as he continues his appeal to* MISS FELLOWES.]

MISS FELLOWES: I've taken a look at those rooms and they'd make a room at the "Y" look like a suite at the Ritz.

SHANNON: Miss Fellowes, I am employed by Blake Tours and so I'm not in a position to tell you quite frankly what mistakes they've made in their advertising brochure. They just don't know Mexico. I do. I know it as well as I know five out of all six continents on the—

MISS FELLOWES: *Continent! Mexico?* You never even studied geography if you—

SHANNON: My degree from Sewanee is *Doctor* of *Divinity*, but for the past ten years geography's been my *specialty*, Miss Fellowes, honey! Name any tourist agency I haven't worked for! You couldn't! I'm only, now, with Blake Tours because I—

MISS FELLOWES: Because you *what?* Couldn't keep your hands off innocent, under-age girls in your—

SHANNON: Now, Miss Fellowes. . . . [*He touches her arm again.*]

MISS FELLOWES: Take your hand off my arm!

SHANNON: For days I've known you were furious and unhappy, but—

MISS FELLOWES: *Oh!* You think it's just *me* that's unhappy! Hauled in that stifling bus over the byways, off the highways, shook up and bumped up so you could get your rake-off, is that what you—

SHANNON: What I know is, all I know is, that you are the *leader* of the *insurrection!*

MISS FELLOWES: All of the girls in this party have dysentery!

SHANNON: That you can't hold me to blame for.

MISS FELLOWES: I *do* hold you to blame for it.

SHANNON: Before we entered Mexico, at New Laredo, Texas, I called you ladies together in the depot on the Texas side of the border and I passed out mimeographed sheets of instructions on what to eat and what *not* to eat, what to drink, what *not* to drink in the—

MISS FELLOWES: It's not *what* we ate but *where* we ate that gave us dysentery!

SHANNON [*shaking his head like a metronome*]: It is not dysentery.

MISS FELLOWES: The result of eating in places that would be condemned by the Board of Health in—

SHANNON: Now wait a minute—

MISS FELLOWES: For disregarding all rules of sanitation.

SHANNON: It is not dysentery, it is not amoebic, it's nothing at all but—

MAXINE: Montezuma's Revenge! That's what we call it.

SHANNON: I even passed out pills. I passed out bottles of Enteroviaform because I knew that some of you ladies would rather be victims of Montezuma's Revenge than spend cinco centavos on bottled water in stations.

MISS FELLOWES: You sold those pills at a profit of fifty cents per bottle.

MAXINE: Hah-hah! [*She knocks off the end of a coconut with the machete, preparing a rum-coco.*]

SHANNON: Now fun is fun, Miss Fellowes, but an accusation like that—

MISS FELLOWES: I *priced* them in *pharmacies*, because I suspected that—

SHANNON: Miss Fellowes, I am a gentleman, and as a gentleman I can't be insulted like this. I mean I can't accept insults of that kind even from a member of a tour that I am conducting. And, Miss Fellowes, I think you might also remember, you might try to remember, that you're speaking to an ordained minister of the Church.

MISS FELLOWES: *De*-frocked! But still trying to pass himself off as a minister!

MAXINE: How about a rum-coco? We give a complimentary rum-coco to all our guests here. [*Her offer is apparently unheard. She shrugs and drinks the rum-coco herself.*]

SHANNON: —Miss Fellowes? In every party there is always one individual that's discontented, that is not satisfied with all I do to make the tour more . . . unique—to make it different from the ordinary, to give it a personal thing, the Shannon touch.

MISS FELLOWES: The gyp touch, the touch of a defrocked minister.

SHANNON: Miss Fellowes, don't, don't, don't . . . do what . . . you're doing! [*He is on the verge of hysteria, he makes some incoherent sounds, gesticulates with clenched fits, then stumbles wildly across the verandah and leans panting for breath against a post.*] Don't! Break! *Human! Pride!*

VOICE FROM DOWN THE HILL [*a very Texan accent*]: Judy? They're taking our luggage!

MISS FELLOWES [*shouting down the hill*]: Girls! Girls! Don't let those boys touch your luggage. Don't let them bring your luggage in this dump!

GIRL'S VOICE [*from below*]: Judy! We can't stop them!

MAXINE: Those kids don't understand English.

MISS FELLOWES [*wild with rage*]: Will you please tell those boys to take that luggage back down to the bus? [*She calls to the party below again.*] Girls! Hold onto your luggage, don't let them take it away! We're going to drive back to A-cap-ul-co! *You hear?*

GIRL'S VOICE: Judy, they want a swim, first!

MISS FELLOWES: I'll be right back. [*She rushes off, shouting at the Mexican boys.*] You! Boys! Muchachos! *You carry that luggage back down!*

[*The voices continue, fading.* SHANNON *moves brokenly across the verandah.* MAXINE *shakes her head.*]

MAXINE: Shannon, give 'em the bus key and let 'em go.

SHANNON: And me do what?

MAXINE: Stay here.

SHANNON: In Fred's old bedroom—yeah, in Fred's old bedroom.

MAXINE: You could do worse.

SHANNON: Could I? Well, then, I'll do worse, I'll . . . do worse.

MAXINE: Aw now, baby.

SHANNON: If I could do worse, I'll do worse. . . . [*He grips the section of railing by the verandah steps and stares with wide, lost eyes. His chest heaves like a spent runner's and he is bathed in sweat.*]

MAXINE: Give me that ignition key. I'll take it down to the driver while you bathe and rest and have a rum-coco, baby.

[SHANNON *simply shakes his head slightly. Harsh bird cries sound in the rain forest. Voices are heard on the path.*]

HANNAH: Nonno, you've lost your sun glasses.

NONNO: No. Took them off. No sun.

[HANNAH *appears at the top of the path, pushing her grandfather,* NONNO, *in a wheelchair. He is a very old man but has a powerful voice for his age and always seems to be shouting something of importance.* NONNO *is a poet and a showman. There is a good kind of pride and he has it, carrying it like a banner wherever he goes. He is immaculately dressed—a linen suit, white as his thick poet's hair; a black string tie; and he is holding a black cane with a gold crook.*]

NONNO: Which way is the sea?

HANNAH: Right down below the hill, Nonno. [*He turns in*

the wheelchair and raises a hand to shield his eyes.] We can't
see it from here. [*The old man is deaf, and she shouts to make
him hear.*]

NONNO: I can feel it and smell it. [*A murmur of wind
sweeps through the rain forest.*] It's the cradle of life. [*He is
shouting, too.*] Life began in the sea.

MAXINE: These two with your party?

SHANNON: No.

MAXINE: They look like a pair of loonies.

SHANNON: Shut up.

[SHANNON *looks at* HANNAH *and* NONNO *steadily, with a re-
lief of tension almost like that of someone going under
hypnosis. The old man still squints down the path, blindly,
but* HANNAH *is facing the verandah with a proud person's
hope of acceptance when it is desperately needed.*]

HANNAH: How do you do.

MAXINE: Hello.

HANNAH: Have you ever tried pushing a gentleman in a
wheelchair uphill through a rain forest?

MAXINE: Nope, and I wouldn't even try it *downhill.*

HANNAH: Well, now that we've made it, I don't regret the
effort. What a view for a painter! [*She looks about her, panting, digging into her shoulder-bag for a handkerchief, aware
that her face is flushed and sweating.*] They told me in town
that this was the ideal place for a painter, and they weren't
—*whew*—exaggerating!

SHANNON: You've got a scratch on your forehead.

HANNAH: Oh, is that what I felt.

SHANNON: Better put iodine on it.

HANNAH: Yes, I'll attend to that—*whew*—later, thank you.

MAXINE: Anything I can do for you?

HANNAH: I'm looking for the manager of the hotel.

MAXINE: Me—speaking.

HANNAH: Oh, *you're* the manager, *good!* How do you do, I'm Hannah Jelkes, Mrs. . . .

MAXINE: Faulk, Maxine Faulk. What can I do for you folks? [*Her tone indicates no desire to do anything for them.*]

HANNAH [*turning quickly to her grandfather*]: Nonno, the manager is a *lady* from the *States*.

[NONNO *lifts a branch of wild orchids from his lap, ceremonially, with the instinctive gallantry of his kind.*]

NONNO [*shouting*]: Give the lady these—botanical curiosities!—you picked on the way up.

HANNAH: I believe they're wild orchids, isn't that what they are?

SHANNON: Laelia tibicina.

HANNAH: Oh!

NONNO: But tell her, Hannah, tell her to keep them in the icebox till after dark, they draw bees in the sun! [*He rubs a sting on his chin with a rueful chuckle.*]

MAXINE: Are you all looking for rooms here?

HANNAH: Yes, we are, but we've come without reservations.

MAXINE: Well, honey, the Costa Verde is closed in September—except for a few special guests, so. . . .

SHANNON: They're special guests, for God's sake.

MAXINE: I thought you said they didn't come with your party.

HANNAH: Please let us be special guests.

MAXINE: *Watch out!*

[NONNO *has started struggling out of the wheelchair.* SHANNON *rushes over to keep him from falling.* HANNAH *has started toward him, too, then seeing that* SHANNON *has caught him, she turns back to* MAXINE.]

HANNAH: In twenty-five years of travel this is the first time we've ever arrived at a place without advance reservations.

MAXINE: Honey, that old man ought to be in a hospital.

HANNAH: Oh, no, no, he just sprained his ankle a little in Taxco this morning. He just needs a good night's rest, he'll be on his feet tomorrow. His recuperative powers are absolutely amazing for someone who is ninety-seven years *young.*

SHANNON: Easy, Grampa. Hang on. [*He is supporting the old man up to the verandah.*] Two steps. One! Two! Now you've made it, Grampa.

[NONNO *keeps chuckling breathlessly as* SHANNON *gets him onto the verandah and into a wicker rocker.*]

HANNAH [*breaking in quickly*]: I can't tell you how much I appreciate your taking us in here now. It's—providential.

MAXINE: Well, I can't send that old man back down the hill—right now—but like I told you the Costa Verde's practically closed in September. I just take in a few folks as a special accommodation and we operate on a special basis this month.

NONNO [*cutting in abruptly and loudly*]: Hannah, tell the lady that my perambulator is temporary. I will soon be ready

to crawl and then to toddle and before long I will be leaping
around here like an—old—mountain—goat, ha-ha-ha-ha. . . .

HANNAH: Yes, I explained that, Grandfather.

NONNO: I don't like being on wheels.

HANNAH: Yes, my grandfather feels that the decline of the
western world began with the invention of the wheel. [*She
laughs heartily, but* MAXINE'S *look is unresponsive.*]

NONNO: And tell the manager . . . the, uh, lady . . . that I
know some hotels don't want to take dogs, cats or monkeys
and some don't even solicit the patronage of infants in their
late nineties who arrive in perambulators with flowers instead
of rattles . . . [*He chuckles with a sort of fearful, slightly
mad quality.* HANNAH *perhaps has the impulse to clap a hand
over his mouth at this moment but must stand there smiling
and smiling and smiling.*] . . . and a brandy flask instead of a
teething ring, but tell her that these, uh, concessions to man's
seventh age are only temporary, and. . . .

HANNAH: Nonno, I told her the wheelchair's because of a
sprained ankle, Nonno!

SHANNON [*to himself*]: Fantastic.

NONNO: And after my siesta, I'll wheel it back down the hill,
I'll kick it back down the hill, right into the sea, and tell her.
. . .

HANNAH: Yes? What, Nonno? [*She has stopped smiling now.
Her tone and her look are frankly desperate.*] What shall I
tell her now, Nonno?

NONNO: Tell her that if she'll forgive my disgraceful lon-
gevity and this . . . temporary decrepitude . . . I will present
her with the last signed . . . compitty [*he means* "copy"] of
my first volume of verse, published in . . . when, Hannah?

HANNAH [*hopelessly*]: The day that President Ulysses S.
Grant was inaugurated, Nonno.

NONNO: *Morning Trumpet!* Where is it—you have it, give it to her right now.

HANNAH: Later, a little later! [*Then she turns to* MAXINE *and* SHANNON.] My grandfather is the poet Jonathan Coffin. He is ninety-seven years *young* and will be ninety-eight years *young* the fifth of next month, October.

MAXINE: Old folks are remarkable, yep. The office phone's ringing—excuse me, I'll be right back. [*She goes around the verandah.*]

NONNO: Did I talk too much?

HANNAH [*quietly, to* SHANNON]: I'm afraid that he did. I don't think she's going to take us.

SHANNON: She'll take you. Don't worry about it.

HANNAH: Nobody would take us in town, and if we don't get in here, I would have to wheel him back down through the rain forest, and then *what,* then *where?* There would just be the road, and no direction to move in, except out to sea—and I doubt that we could make it divide before us.

SHANNON: That won't be necessary. I have a little influence with the patrona.

HANNAH: Oh, then, do use it, please. Her eyes said *no* in big blue capital letters.

[SHANNON *pours some water from a pitcher on the verandah and hands it to the old man.*]

NONNO: What is this—libation?

SHANNON: Some icewater, Grampa.

HANNAH: Oh, that's kind of you. Thank you. I'd better give him a couple of salt tablets to wash down with it. [*Briskly she removes a bottle from her shoulder-bag.*] Won't you have some? I see you're perspiring, too. You have to be careful not to become dehydrated in the hot seasons under the Tropic of Cancer.

SHANNON [*pouring another glass of water*]: Are you a little *financially* dehydrated, too?

HANNAH: That's right. Bone-dry, and I think the patrona suspects it. It's a logical assumption, since I pushed him up here myself, and the patrona has the look of a very logical woman. I am sure she knows that we couldn't afford to hire the taxi driver to help us up here.

MAXINE [*calling from the back*]: Pancho?

HANNAH: A woman's practicality when she's managing something is harder than a man's for another woman to cope with, so if you have influence with her, please do use it. Please try to convince her that my grandfather will be on his feet tomorrow, if not tonight, and with any luck whatsoever, the money situation will be solved just as quickly. Oh, here she comes back, do help us!

[*Involuntarily,* HANNAH *seizes hold of* SHANNON'S *wrist as* MAXINE *stalks back onto the verandah, still shouting for* PANCHO. *The Mexican boy reappears, sucking a juicy peeled mango—its juice running down his chin onto his throat.*]

MAXINE: Pancho, run down to the beach and tell Herr Fahrenkopf that the German Embassy's waiting on the phone for him. [PANCHO *stares at her blankly until she repeats the order in Spanish.*] Dile a Herr Fahrenkopf que la embajada alemana lo llama al teléfono. Corre, corre! [PANCHO *starts indolently down the path, still sucking noisily on the mango.*] I said *run!* Corre, corre! [*He goes into a leisurely loping pace and disappears through the foliage.*]

HANNAH: What graceful people they are!

MAXINE: Yeah, they're graceful like cats, and just as dependable, too.

HANNAH: Shall we, uh, . . . *register* now?

MAXINE: You all can register later but I'll have to collect six dollars from you first if you want to put your names in the pot for supper. That's how I've got to operate here out of season.

HANNAH: Six? Dollars?

MAXINE: Yeah, three each. In season we operate on the continental plan but out of season like this we change to the modified American plan.

HANNAH: Oh, what is the, uh . . . modification of it? [*She gives* SHANNON *a quick glance of appeal as she stalls for time, but his attention has turned inward as the bus horn blows down the hill.*]

MAXINE: Just two meals are included instead of all three.

HANNAH [*moving closer to* SHANNON *and raising her voice*]: Breakfast and dinner?

MAXINE: A continental breakfast and a cold lunch.

SHANNON [*aside*]: Yeah, very cold—cracked ice—if you crack it yourself.

HANNAH [*reflectively*]: Not dinner.

MAXINE: No! Not dinner.

HANNAH: Oh, I see, uh, but . . . we, uh, operate on a special basis ourselves. I'd better explain it to you.

MAXINE: How do you mean "operate,"—on what "basis"?

HANNAH: Here's our card. I think you may have heard of us. [*She presents the card to* MAXINE.] We've had a good many write-ups. My grandfather is the oldest living and practicing poet. *And* he gives recitations. I . . . paint . . . water colors and I'm a "quick sketch artist." We travel together. We pay our way as we go by my grandfather's recitations and the sale of my water colors and quick character sketches in charcoal or pastel.

SHANNON [*to himself*]: I have fever.

HANNAH: I usually pass among the tables at lunch and dinner in a hotel. I wear an artist's smock—picturesquely dabbed with paint—wide Byronic collar and flowing silk tie. I don't push myself on people. I just display my work and smile at them sweetly and if they invite me to do so sit down to make a quick character sketch in pastel or charcoal. If not? Smile sweetly and go on.

SHANNON: What does Grandpa do?

HANNAH: We pass among the tables together slowly. I introduce him as the world's oldest living and practicing poet. If invited, he gives a recitation of a poem. Unfortunately all of his poems were written a long time ago. But do you know, he has started a new poem? For the first time in twenty years he's started another poem!

SHANNON: Hasn't finished it yet?

HANNAH: He still has inspiration, but his power of concentration has weakened a little, of course.

MAXINE: Right now he's not concentrating.

SHANNON: Grandpa's catchin' forty winks. Grampa? Let's hit the sack.

MAXINE: Now wait a minute. I'm going to call a taxi for these folks to take them back to town.

HANNAH: Please don't do that. We tried every hotel in town and they wouldn't take us. I'm afraid I have to place myself at your . . . mercy.

[*With infinite gentleness* SHANNON *has roused the old man and is leading him into one of the cubicles back of the*

*verandah. Distant cries of bathers are heard from the
beach. The afternoon light is fading very fast now as the
sun has dropped behind an island hilltop out to sea.]*

MAXINE: Looks like you're in for one night. Just one.

HANNAH: Thank you.

MAXINE: The old man's in number 4. You take 3. Where's
your luggage—no luggage?

HANNAH: I hid it behind some palmettos at the foot of
the path.

SHANNON [*shouting to* PANCHO]: Bring up her luggage. Tu,
flojo . . . las maletas . . . baja las palmas. Vamos! [*The
Mexican boys rush down the path.*] Maxine honey, would
you cash a postdated check for me?

MAXINE [*shrewdly*]: Yeah—mañana, maybe.

SHANNON: Thanks—generosity is the cornerstone of your
nature.

[MAXINE *utters her one-note bark of a laugh as she marches
around the corner of the verandah.*]

HANNAH: I'm dreadfully afraid my grandfather had a
slight stroke in those high passes through the sierras. [*She
says this with the coolness of someone saying that it may
rain before nightfall. An instant later, a long, long sigh of
wind sweeps the hillside. The bathers are heard shouting
below.*]

SHANNON: Very old people get these little "cerebral accidents," as they call them. They're not regular strokes, they're
just little cerebral . . . incidents. The symptoms clear up so
quickly that sometimes the old people don't even know
they've had them.

[*They exchange this quiet talk without looking at each
other. The Mexican boys crash back through the bushes*

at the top of the path, bearing some pieces of ancient luggage fantastically plastered with hotel and travel stickers indicating a vast range of wandering. The boys deposit the luggage near the steps.]

SHANNON: How many times have you been around the world?

HANNAH: Almost as many times as the world's been around the sun, and I feel as if I had gone the whole way on foot.

SHANNON [*picking up her luggage*]: What's your cell number?

HANNAH [*smiling faintly*]: I believe she said it was cell number 3.

SHANNON: She probably gave you the one with the leaky roof. [*He carries the bags into the cubicle.* MAXINE *is visible to the audience only as she appears outside the door to her office on the wing of the verandah.*] But you won't find out till it rains and then it'll be too late to do much about it but swim out of it. [HANNAH *laughs wanly. Her fatigue is now very plain.* SHANNON *comes back out with her luggage.*] Yep, she gave you the one with the leaky roof so you take mine and. . . .

HANNAH: Oh, no, no, Mr. Shannon, I'll find a dry spot if it rains.

MAXINE [*from around the corner of the verandah*]: Shannon!

[*A bit of pantomime occurs between* HANNAH *and* SHANNON. *He wants to put her luggage in cubicle number 5. She catches hold of his arm, indicating by gesture toward the back that it is necessary to avoid displeasing the proprietor.* MAXINE *shouts his name louder.* SHANNON *surrenders to* HANNAH'S *pleading and puts her luggage back in the leaky cubicle number 3.*]

HANNAH: Thank you so much, Mr. Shannon. [*She dis-*

appears behind the mosquito netting. MAXINE *advances to the verandah angle as* SHANNON *starts toward his own cubicle.*]

MAXINE [*mimicking* HANNAH's *voice*]: "Thank you so much, Mr. Shannon."

SHANNON: Don't be bitchy. Some people say thank you sincerely. [*He goes past her and down the steps from the end of the verandah.*] I'm going down for a swim now.

MAXINE: The water's blood temperature this time of day.

SHANNON: Yeah, well, I have a fever so it'll seem cooler to me. [*He crosses rapidly to the jungle path leading to the beach.*]

MAXINE [*following him*]: Wait for me, I'll. . . .

[*She means she will go down with him, but he ignores her call and disappears into the foliage.* MAXINE *shrugs angrily and goes back onto the verandah. She faces out, gripping the railing tightly and glaring into the blaze of the sunset as if it were a personal enemy. Then the ocean breathes a long cooling breath up the hill, as* NONNO's *voice is heard from his cubicle.*]

NONNO:

> How calmly does the orange branch
> Observe the sky begin to blanch,
> Without a cry, without a prayer,
> With no expression of despair. . . .

[*And from a beach cantina in the distance a marimba band is heard playing a popular song of that summer of 1940, "Palabras de Mujer"—which means "Words of Women."*]

SLOW DIM OUT AND SLOW CURTAIN

Act Two

Several hours later: near sunset.
The scene is bathed in a deep
golden, almost coppery light;
the heavy tropical foliage gleams with wetness from a recent
rain.

MAXINE *comes around the turn of the verandah. To the*
formalities of evening she has made the concession of chang-
ing from levis to clean white cotton pants, and from a blue
work shirt to a pink one. She is about to set up the folding
cardtables for the evening meal which is served on the
verandah. All the while she is talking, she is setting up tables,
etc.

MAXINE: Miss Jelkes?

[HANNAH *lifts the mosquito net over the door of cubicle*
number 3.]

HANNAH: Yes, Mrs. Faulk?

MAXINE: Can I speak to you while I set up these tables
for supper?

HANNAH: Of course, you may. I wanted to speak to you,
too. [*She comes out. She is now wearing her artist's smock.*]

MAXINE: Good.

HANNAH: I just wanted to ask you if there's a tub-bath
Grandfather could use. A shower is fine for me—I prefer a
shower to a tub—but for my grandfather there is some danger
of falling down in a shower and at his age, although he says
he is made out of India rubber, a broken hipbone would be
a very serious matter, so I. . . .

MAXINE: What I wanted to say is I called up the Casa de Huéspedes about you and your Grampa, and I can get you in there.

HANNAH: Oh, but we don't want to *move!*

MAXINE: The Costa Verde isn't the right place for you. Y'see, we cater to folks that like to rough it a little, and— well, frankly, we cater to younger people.

[HANNAH *has started unfolding a cardtable.*]

HANNAH: Oh yes . . . uh . . . well . . . the, uh, Casa de Huéspedes, that means a, uh, sort of a rooming house, Mrs. Faulk?

MAXINE: Boarding house. They feed you, they'll even feed you on credit.

HANNAH: Where is it located?

MAXINE: It has a central location. You could get a doctor there quick if the old man took sick on you. You got to think about that.

HANNAH: Yes, I—[*She nods gravely, more to herself than* MAXINE.]—I *have* thought about that, but. . . .

MAXINE: What are you doing?

HANNAH: Making myself useful.

MAXINE: Don't do that. I don't accept help from guests here.

[HANNAH *hesitates, but goes on setting the tables.*]

HANNAH: Oh, please, let me. Knife and fork on one side, spoon on the . . . ? [*Her voice dies out.*]

MAXINE: Just put the plates on the napkins so they don't blow away.

HANNAH: Yes, it is getting breezy on the verandah. [*She continues setting the table.*]

MAXINE: Hurricane winds are already hitting up coast.

HANNAH: We've been through several typhoons in the Orient. Sometimes *outside* disturbances like that are an almost welcome distraction from *inside* disturbances, aren't they? [*This is said almost to herself. She finishes putting the plates on the paper napkins.*] When do you want us to leave here, Mrs. Faulk?

MAXINE: The boys'll move you in my station wagon tomorrow—no charge for the service.

HANNAH: That is very kind of you. [MAXINE *starts away.*] Mrs. Faulk?

MAXINE [*turning back to her with obvious reluctance*]: Huh?

HANNAH: Do you know jade?

MAXINE: Jade?

HANNAH: Yes.

MAXINE: Why?

HANNAH: I have a small but interesting collection of jade pieces. I asked if you know jade because in jade it's the craftsmanship, the carving of the jade, that's most important about it. [*She has removed a jade ornament from her blouse.*] This one, for instance—a miracle of carving. Tiny as it is, it has two figures carved on it—the legendary Prince Ahk and Princess Angh, and a heron flying above them. The artist that carved it probably received for this miraculously delicate workmanship, well, I would say perhaps the price of a month's supply of rice for his family, but the merchant who employed him sold it, I would guess, for at least three hundred pounds sterling to an English lady who got tired of it and gave it to me, perhaps because I painted her not as she was at that

time but as I could see she must have looked in her youth.
Can you see the carving?

MAXINE: Yeah, honey, but I'm not operating a hock shop
here, I'm trying to run a hotel.

HANNAH: I know, but couldn't you just accept it as security
for a few days' stay here?

MAXINE: You're completely broke, are you?

HANNAH: Yes, we are—completely.

MAXINE: You say that like you're proud of it.

HANNAH: I'm not proud of it or ashamed of it either. It
just happens to be what's happened to us, which has never
happened before in all our travels.

MAXINE [grudgingly]: You're telling the truth, I reckon,
but I told you the truth, too, when I told you, when you
came here, that I had just lost my husband and he'd left
me in such a financial hole that if living didn't mean more
to me than money, I'd might as well have been dropped in
the ocean with him.

HANNAH: Ocean?

MAXINE [peacefully philosophical about it]: I carried out
his burial instructions exactly. Yep, my husband, Fred Faulk,
was the greatest game fisherman on the West Coast of Mexico—he'd racked up unbeatable records in sailfish, tarpon,
kingfish, barracuda—and on his deathbed, last week, he requested to be dropped in the sea, yeah, right out there in
that bay, not even sewed up in canvas, just in his fisherman
outfit. So now old Freddie the Fisherman is feeding the fish
—fishes' revenge on old Freddie. How about that, I ask you?

HANNAH [regarding MAXINE sharply]: I doubt that he regrets
it.

MAXINE: I do. It gives me the shivers.

[*She is distracted by the German party singing a marching song on the path up from the beach.* SHANNON *appears at the top of the path, a wet beachrobe clinging to him.* MAXINE'S *whole concentration shifts abruptly to him. She freezes and blazes with it like an exposed power line. For a moment the "hot light" is concentrated on her tense, furious figure.* HANNAH *provides a visual counterpoint. She clenches her eyes shut for a moment, and when they open, it is on a look of stoical despair of the refuge she has unsuccessfully fought for. Then* SHANNON *approaches the verandah and the scene is his.*]

SHANNON: Here they come up, your conquerors of the world, Maxine honey, singing "Horst Wessel." [*He chuckles fiercely, and starts toward the verandah steps.*]

MAXINE: Shannon, wash that sand off you before you come on the verandah.

[*The Germans are heard singing the "Horst Wessel" marching song. Soon they appear, trooping up from the beach like an animated canvas by Rubens. They are all nearly nude, pinked and bronzed by the sun. The women have decked themselves with garlands of pale green seaweed, glistening wet, and the Munich-opera bridegroom is blowing on a great conch shell. His father-in-law, the tank manufacturer, has his portable radio, which is still transmitting a shortwave broadcast about the Battle of Britain, now at its climax.*]

HILDA [*capering, astride her rubber horse*]: Horsey, horsey, horsey!

HERR FAHRENKOPF [*ecstatically*]: London is burning, the heart of London's on fire! [WOLFGANG *turns a handspring onto the verandah and walks on his hands a few paces, then tumbles over with a great whoop.* MAXINE *laughs delightedly with the Germans.*] Beer, beer, beer!

FRAU FAHRENKOPF: Tonight champagne!

[*The euphoric horseplay and shouting continue as they*

gambol around the turn of the verandah. SHANNON *has come onto the porch.* MAXINE'S *laughter dies out a little sadly, with envy.*]

SHANNON: You're turning this place into the Mexican Berchtesgaden, Maxine honey?

MAXINE: I told you to wash that sand off. [*Shouts for beer from the Germans draw her around the verandah corner.*]

HANNAH: Mr. Shannon, do you happen to know the Casa de Huéspedes, or anything about it, I mean? [SHANNON *stares at her somewhat blankly.*] We are, uh, thinking of . . . *moving* there tomorrow. Do you, uh, recommend it?

SHANNON: I recommend it along with the Black Hole of Calcutta and the Siberian salt mines.

HANNAH [*nodding reflectively*]: I suspected as much. Mr. Shannon, in your touring party, do you think there might be anyone interested in my water colors? Or in my character sketches?

SHANNON: I doubt it. I doubt that they're corny enough to please my ladies. *Oh-oh! Great Caesar's ghost.* . . .

[*This exclamation is prompted by the shrill, approaching call of his name.* CHARLOTTE *appears from the rear, coming from the hotel annex, and rushes like a teen-age Medea toward the verandah.* SHANNON *ducks into his cubicle, slamming the door so quickly that a corner of the mosquito netting is caught and sticks out, flirtatiously.* CHARLOTTE *rushes onto the verandah.*]

CHARLOTTE: *Larry!*

HANNAH: Are you looking for someone, dear?

CHARLOTTE: Yeah, the man conducting our tour, Larry Shannon.

HANNAH: Oh, Mr. Shannon. I think he went down to the beach.

CHARLOTTE: I just now saw him coming up from the beach. [*She is tense and trembling, and her eyes keep darting up and down the verandah.*]

HANNAH: Oh. Well. . . . But. . . .

CHARLOTTE: Larry? Larry! [*Her shouts startle the rain-forest birds into a clamorous moment.*]

HANNAH: Would you like to leave a message for him, dear?

CHARLOTTE: No. I'm staying right here till he comes out of wherever he's hiding.

HANNAH: Why don't you just sit down, dear. I'm an artist, a painter. I was just sorting out my water colors and sketches in this portfolio, and look what I've come across. [*She selects a sketch and holds it up.*]

SHANNON [*from inside his cubicle*]: Oh, God!

CHARLOTTE [*darting to the cubicle*]: Larry, let me in there!

[*She beats on the door of the cubicle as* HERR FAHRENKOPF *comes around the verandah with his portable radio. He is bug-eyed with excitement over the news broadcast in German.*]

HANNAH: Guten abend.

[HERR FAHRENKOPF *jerks his head with a toothy grin, raising a hand for silence.* HANNAH *nods agreeably and approaches him with her portfolio of drawings. He maintains the grin as she displays one picture after another.* HANNAH *is uncertain whether the grin is for the pictures or the news broadcast. He stares at the pictures, jerking his head from time to time. It is rather like the pantomime of showing lantern slides.*]

CHARLOTTE [*suddenly crying out again*]: Larry, open this door and let me in! I know you're in there, Larry!

HERR FAHRENKOPF: Silence, please, for one moment! This is a recording of Der Führer addressing the Reichstag just . . . [*He glances at his wristwatch.*] . . . eight hours ago, today, transmitted by Deutsches Nachrichtenbüro to Mexico City. Please! Quiet, bitte!

[*A human voice like a mad dog's bark emerges from the static momentarily.* CHARLOTTE *goes on pounding on* SHANNON'S *door.* HANNAH *suggests in pantomime that they go to the back verandah, but* HERR FAHRENKOPF *despairs of hearing the broadcast. As he rises to leave, the light catches his polished glasses so that he appears for a moment to have electric light bulbs in his forehead. Then he ducks his head in a genial little bow and goes out beyond the verandah, where he performs some muscle-flexing movements of a formalized nature, like the preliminary stances of Japanese Suma wrestlers.*]

HANNAH: May I show you my work on the other verandah?

[HANNAH *had started to follow* HERR FAHRENKOPF *with her portfolio, but the sketches fall out, and she stops to gather them from the floor with the sad, preoccupied air of a lovely child picking flowers.*]

[SHANNON'S *head slowly, furtively, appears through the window of his cubicle. He draws quickly back as* CHARLOTTE *darts that way, stepping on* HANNAH'S *spilt sketches.* HANNAH *utters a soft cry of protest, which is drowned by* CHARLOTTE'S *renewed clamor.*]

CHARLOTTE: Larry, Larry, Judy's looking for me. Let me come in, Larry, before she finds me here!

SHANNON: You can't come in. Stop shouting and I'll come out.

CHARLOTTE: All right, come out.

SHANNON: Stand back from the door so I *can*.

[*She moves a little aside and he emerges from his cubicle like a man entering a place of execution. He leans against the wall, mopping the sweat off his face with a handkerchief.*]

SHANNON: How does Miss Fellowes know what happened that night? Did you tell her?

CHARLOTTE: I didn't tell her, she guessed.

SHANNON: Guessing isn't knowing. If she is just guessing, that means she doesn't know—I mean if you're not lying, if you didn't tell her.

[*HANNAH has finished picking up her drawings and moves quietly over to the far side of the verandah.*]

CHARLOTTE: Don't talk to me like that.

SHANNON: Don't complicate my life now, please, for God's sake, don't complicate my life now.

CHARLOTTE: Why have you changed like this?

SHANNON: I have a fever. Don't complicate my . . . fever.

CHARLOTTE: You act like you hated me now.

SHANNON: You're going to get me kicked out of Blake Tours, Charlotte.

CHARLOTTE: Judy is, not me.

SHANNON: Why did you sing "I Love You Truly" at me?

CHARLOTTE: Because I do love you truly!

SHANNON: Honey girl, don't you know that nothing worse could happen to a girl in your, your . . . unstable condition . . .

than to get emotionally mixed up with a man in my unstable condition, huh?

CHARLOTTE: No, no, no, I—

SHANNON [*cutting through*]: Two unstable conditions can set a whole world on fire, can blow it up, past repair, and that is just as true between two people as it's true between. . . .

CHARLOTTE: All I know is you've got to marry me, Larry, after what happened between us in Mexico City!

SHANNON: A man in my condition can't marry, it isn't decent or legal. He's lucky if he can even hold onto his job. [*He keeps catching hold of her hands and plucking them off his shoulders.*] I'm almost out of my mind, can't you see that, honey?

CHARLOTTE: I don't believe you don't love me.

SHANNON: Honey, it's almost impossible for anybody to believe they're not loved by someone they believe they love, but, honey, I love *nobody*. I'm like that, it isn't my fault. When I brought you home that night I told you goodnight in the hall, just kissed you on the cheek like the little girl that you are, but the instant I opened my door, you rushed into my room and I couldn't get you out of it, not even when I, oh God, tried to scare you out of it by, oh God, don't you remember?

[MISS FELLOWES' *voice is heard from back of the hotel calling,* "Charlotte!"]

CHARLOTTE: Yes, I remember that after making love to me, you hit me, Larry, you struck me in the face, and you twisted my arm to make me kneel on the floor and pray with you for forgiveness.

SHANNON: I do that, I do that always when I, when . . . I don't have a dime left in my nervous emotional bank account —I can't write a check on it, now.

CHARLOTTE: Larry, let me help you!

MISS FELLOWES [*approaching*]: Charlotte, Charlotte, Charlie!

CHARLOTTE: Help me and let me help you!

SHANNON: The helpless can't help the helpless!

CHARLOTTE: Let me in, Judy's coming!

SHANNON: Let me go. Go away!

[*He thrusts her violently back and rushes into his cubicle, slamming and bolting the door—though the gauze netting is left sticking out. As* MISS FELLOWES *charges onto the verandah,* CHARLOTTE *runs into the next cubicle, and* HANNAH *moves over from where she has been watching and meets her in the center.*]

MISS FELLOWES: Shannon, Shannon! Where are you?

HANNAH: I think Mr. Shannon has gone down to the beach.

MISS FELLOWES: Was Charlotte Goodall with him? A young blonde girl in our party—was she with him?

HANNAH: No, nobody was with him, he was completely alone.

MISS FELLOWES: I heard a door slam.

HANNAH: That was mine.

MISS FELLOWES [*pointing to the door with the gauze sticking out*]: Is this yours?

HANNAH: Yes, mine. I rushed out to catch the sunset.

[*At this moment* MISS FELLOWES *hears* CHARLOTTE *sobbing in* HANNAH's *cubicle. She throws the door open.*]

MISS FELLOWES: Charlotte! Come out of there, Charlie! [*She has seized* CHARLOTTE *by the wrist.*] What's your word worth—nothing? You promised you'd stay away from him! [CHARLOTTE *frees her arm, sobbing bitterly.* MISS FELLOWES *seizes her again, tighter, and starts dragging her away*.] I have talked to your father about this man by long distance and he's getting out a warrant for his arrest, if he dare try coming back to the States after this!

CHARLOTTE: I don't care.

MISS FELLOWES: I do! I'm responsible for you.

CHARLOTTE: I don't want to go back to Texas!

MISS FELLOWES: Yes, you do! And you will!

[*She takes* CHARLOTTE *firmly by the arm and drags her away behind the hotel.* HANNAH *comes out of her cubicle, where she had gone when* MISS FELLOWES *pulled* CHARLOTTE *out of it.*]

SHANNON [*from his cubicle*]: Ah, God. . . .

[HANNAH *crosses to his cubicle and knocks by the door*.]

HANNAH: The coast is clear now, Mr. Shannon.

[SHANNON *does not answer or appear. She sets down her portfolio to pick up* NONNO'S *white linen suit, which she had pressed and hung on the verandah. She crosses to his cubicle with it, and calls in.*]

HANNAH: Nonno? It's almost time for supper! There's going to be a lovely, stormy sunset in a few minutes.

NONNO [*from within*]: Coming!

HANNAH: So is Christmas, Nonno.

NONNO: So is the Fourth of July!

HANNAH: We're past the Fourth of July. Hallowe'en comes next and then Thanksgiving. I hope you'll come forth sooner.

[*She lifts the gauze net over his cubicle door.*] Here's your suit, I've pressed it. [*She enters the cubicle.*]

NONNO: It's mighty dark in here, Hannah.

HANNAH: I'll turn the light on for you.

[SHANNON *comes out of his cubicle, like the survivor of a plane crash, bringing out with him several pieces of his clerical garb. The black heavy silk bib is loosely fastened about his panting, sweating chest. He hangs over it a heavy gold cross with an amethyst center and attempts to fasten on a starched round collar. Now* HANNAH *comes back out of* NONNO'S *cubicle, adjusting the flowing silk tie which goes with her "artist" costume. For a moment they both face front, adjusting their two outfits. They are like two actors in a play which is about to fold on the road, preparing gravely for a performance which may be the last one.*]

HANNAH [*glancing at* SHANNON]: Are you planning to conduct church services of some kind here tonight, Mr. Shannon?

SHANNON: Goddamit, please help me with this! [*He means the round collar.*]

HANNAH [*crossing behind him*]: If you're not going to conduct a church service, why get into that uncomfortable outfit?

SHANNON: Because I've been accused of being defrocked and of lying about it, that's why. I want to show the ladies that I'm still a clocked—*frocked!*—minister of the. . . .

HANNAH: Isn't that lovely gold cross enough to convince the ladies?

SHANNON: No, they know I redeemed it from a Mexico City pawnshop, and they suspect that that's where I got it in the first place.

HANNAH: Hold still just a minute. [*She is behind him, trying to fasten the collar.*] There now, let's hope it stays on.

The buttonhole is so frayed I'm afraid that it won't hold the button. [*Her fear is instantly confirmed: the button pops out.*]

SHANNON: Where'd it go?

HANNAH: Here, right under. . . .

[*She picks it up.* SHANNON *rips the collar off, crumples it and hurls it off the verandah. Then he falls into the hammock, panting and twisting.* HANNAH *quietly opens her sketch pad and begins to sketch him. He doesn't at first notice what she is doing.*]

HANNAH [*as she sketches*]: How long have you been inactive in the, uh, Church, Mr. Shannon?

SHANNON: What's that got to do with the price of rice in China?

HANNAH [*gently*]: Nothing.

SHANNON: What's it got to do with the price of coffee beans in Brazil?

HANNAH: I retract the question. With apologies.

SHANNON: To answer your question politely, I have been inactive in the Church for all but one year since I was ordained a minister of the Church.

HANNAH [*sketching rapidly and moving forward a bit to see his face better*]: Well, that's quite a sabbatical, Mr. Shannon.

SHANNON: Yeah, that's . . . quite a . . . sabbatical.

[NONNO'S *voice is heard from his cubicle repeating a line of poetry several times.*]

SHANNON: Is your grandfather talking to himself in there?

HANNAH: No, he composes out loud. He has to commit his

lines to memory because he can't see to write them or read them.

SHANNON: Sounds like he's stuck on one line.

HANNAH: Yes. I'm afraid his memory is failing. Memory failure is his greatest dread. [*She says this almost coolly, as if it didn't matter.*]

SHANNON: Are you drawing me?

HANNAH: Trying to. You're a very difficult subject. When the Mexican painter Siqueiros did his portrait of the American poet Hart Crane he had to paint him with closed eyes because he couldn't paint his eyes open—there was too much suffering in them and he couldn't paint it.

SHANNON: Sorry, but I'm not going to close my eyes for you. I'm hypnotizing myself—at least trying to—by looking at the light on the orange tree . . . leaves.

HANNAH: That's all right. I can paint your eyes open.

SHANNON: I had one parish one year and then I wasn't defrocked but I was . . . locked out of my church.

HANNAH: Oh . . . Why did they lock you out of it?

SHANNON: Fornication and heresy . . . in the same week.

HANNAH [*sketching rapidly*]: What were the circumstances of the . . . uh . . . first offense?

SHANNON: Yeah, the fornication came first, preceded the heresy by several days. A very young Sunday-school teacher asked to see me privately in my study. A pretty little thing—no chance in the world—only child, and both of her parents were spinsters, almost identical spinsters wearing clothes of the opposite sexes. Fooling some of the people some of the time but not me—none of the time. . . . [*He is pacing the verandah with gathering agitation, and the all-inclusive mock-*

ery that his guilt produces.] Well, she declared herself to me—wildly.

HANNAH: A declaration of love?

SHANNON: Don't make *fun* of me, honey!

HANNAH: I wasn't.

SHANNON: The natural, or unnatural, attraction of one . . . lunatic for . . . another . . . that's all it was. I was the goddamnedest prig in those days that even I could imagine. I said, let's kneel down together and pray and we did, we knelt down, but all of a sudden the kneeling position turned to a reclining position on the rug of my study and . . . When we got up? I struck her. Yes, I did, I struck her in the face and called her a damned little tramp. So she ran home. I heard the next day she'd cut herself with her father's straightblade razor. Yeah, the paternal spinster shaved.

HANNAH: Fatally?

SHANNON: Just broke the skin surface enough to bleed a little, but it made a scandal.

HANNAH: Yes, I can imagine that it . . . provoked some comment.

SHANNON: That it did, it did that. [*He pauses a moment in his fierce pacing as if the recollection still appalled him.*] So the next Sunday when I climbed into the pulpit and looked down over all of those smug, disapproving, accusing faces uplifted, I had an impulse to shake them—so I shook them. I had a prepared sermon—meek, apologetic—I threw it away, tossed it into the chancel. Look here, I said, I shouted, I'm tired of conducting services in praise and worship of a senile delinquent—yeah, that's what I said, I shouted! All your Western theologies, the whole mythology of them, are based on the concept of God as a *senile delinquent* and, by God, I will not and cannot continue to conduct services in praise and worship of this, this . . . this. . . .

HANNAH [*quietly*]: Senile delinquent?

SHANNON: Yeah, this angry, petulant old man. I mean he's represented like a bad-tempered childish old, old, sick, peevish man—I mean like the sort of old man in a nursing home that's putting together a jigsaw puzzle and can't put it together and gets furious at it and kicks over the table. Yes, I tell you they *do* that, all our theologies do it—accuse God of being a cruel, senile delinquent, blaming the world and brutally punishing all he created for his own faults in construction, and then, ha-ha, yeah—a thunderstorm broke that Sunday. . . .

HANNAH: You mean *outside* the church?

SHANNON: Yep, it was wilder than I was! And out they slithered, they slithered out of their pews to their shiny black cockroach sedans, ha-ha, and I shouted after them, hell, I even followed them halfway out of the church, shouting after them as they. . . . [*He stops with a gasp for breath.*]

HANNAH: Slithered out?

SHANNON: I shouted after them, go on, go home and close your house windows, all your windows and doors, against the truth about God!

HANNAH: Oh, my heavens. Which is just what they did—poor things.

SHANNON: Miss Jelkes honey, Pleasant Valley, Virginia, was an exclusive suburb of a large city and these poor things were not poor—materially speaking.

HANNAH [*smiling a bit*]: What was the, uh, upshot of it?

SHANNON: Upshot of it? Well, I wasn't defrocked. I was just locked out of the church in Pleasant Valley, Virginia, and put in a nice little private asylum to recuperate from a complete nervous breakdown as they preferred to regard it, and then, and then I . . . I entered my present line—tours of God's world conducted by a minister of God with a cross and a round collar to prove it. Collecting evidence!

HANNAH: Evidence of what, Mr. Shannon?

SHANNON [*a touch shyly now*]: My personal idea of God, not as a senile delinquent, but as a. . . .

HANNAH: Incomplete sentence.

SHANNON: It's going to storm tonight—a terrific electric storm. Then you will see the Reverend T. Lawrence Shannon's conception of God Almighty paying a visit to the world he created. I want to go back to the Church and preach the gospel of God as Lightning and Thunder . . . and also stray dogs vivisected and . . . and . . . and. . . . [*He points out suddenly toward the sea.*] That's him! There he is now! [*He is pointing out at a blaze, a majestic apocalypse of gold light, shafting the sky as the sun drops into the Pacific.*] His oblivious majesty—and *here I am* on this . . . dilapidated verandah of a cheap hotel, out of season, in a country caught and destroyed in its flesh and corrupted in its spirit by its gold-hungry Conquistadors that bore the flag of the Inquisition along with the Cross of Christ. Yes . . . and. . . . [*There is a pause.*]

HANNAH: Mr. Shannon . . . ?

SHANNON: Yes . . . ?

HANNAH [*smiling a little*]: I have a strong feeling you will go back to the Church with this evidence you've been collecting, but when you do and it's a black Sunday morning, look out over the congregation, over the smug, complacent faces for a few old, very old faces, looking up at you, as you begin your sermon, with eyes like a piercing cry for something to still look up to, something to still believe in. And then I think you'll not shout what you say you shouted that black Sunday in Pleasant Valley, Virginia. I think you will throw away the violent, furious sermon, you'll toss *it* into the chancel, and talk about . . . no, maybe talk about . . . nothing . . . just. . . .

SHANNON: What?

HANNAH: Lead them beside still waters because you know how badly they need the still waters, Mr. Shannon.

[*There is a moment of silence between them.*]

SHANNON: Lemme see that thing. [*He seizes the sketch pad from her and is visibly impressed by what he sees. There is another moment which is prolonged to* HANNAH'S *embarrassment.*]

HANNAH: Where did you say the patrona put your party of ladies?

SHANNON: She had her . . . Mexican concubines put their luggage in the annex.

HANNAH: Where is the annex?

SHANNON: Right down the hill back of here, but all of my ladies except the teen-age Medea and the older Medea have gone out in a glass-bottomed boat to observe the . . . submarine marvels.

HANNAH: Well, when they come back to the annex they're going to observe my water colors with some marvelous submarine prices marked on the mattings.

SHANNON: By God, you're a hustler, aren't you, you're a fantastic cool hustler.

HANNAH: Yes, like *you*, Mr. Shannon. [*She gently removes her sketch pad from his grasp.*] Oh, Mr. Shannon, if Nonno, Grandfather, comes out of his cell number 4 before I get back, will you please look out for him for me? I won't be longer than three shakes of a lively sheep's tail. [*She snatches up her portfolio and goes briskly off the verandah.*]

SHANNON: Fantastic, absolutely fantastic.

[*There is a windy sound in the rain forest and a flicker of gold light like a silent scattering of gold coins on the verandah; then the sound of shouting voices. The*

*Mexican boys appear with a wildly agitated creature—a
captive iguana tied up in a shirt. They crouch down by the
cactus clumps that are growing below the verandah and
hitch the iguana to a post with a piece of rope.* MAXINE *is
attracted by the commotion and appears on the verandah
above them.*]

PEDRO: Tenemos fiesta!*

PANCHO: Comeremos bien.

PEDRO: Dámela, dámela! Yo la ataré.

PANCHO: *Yo* la cojí—*yo* la ataré!

PEDRO: Lo que vas a *hacer* es dejarla escapar.

MAXINE: Ammarla fuerte! Ole, ole! No la dejes escapar.
Déjala moverse! [*to* SHANNON] They caught an iguana.

SHANNON: I've noticed they did that, Maxine.

[*She is holding her drink deliberately close to him. The
Germans have heard the commotion and crowd onto the
verandah.* FRAU FAHRENKOPF *rushes over to* MAXINE.]

FRAU FAHRENKOPF: What is this? What's going on? A snake?
Did they catch a snake?

MAXINE: No. *Lizard.*

FRAU FAHRENKOPF [*with exaggerated revulsion*]: Ouuu . . .
lizard! [*She strikes a grotesque attitude of terror as if she were
threatened by Jack the Ripper.*]

SHANNON [*to* MAXINE]: You like iguana meat, don't you?

FRAU FAHRENKOPF: Eat? *Eat?* A big *lizard?*

---

* We're going to have a feast! / We'll eat good. / Give it to me!
I'll tie it up. / *I* caught it—*I'll* tie it up! / You'll only let it get away.
/ Tie it up tight! Ole, ole! Don't let it get away. Give it enough room!

MAXINE: Yep, they're mighty good eating—taste like white meat of chicken.

[FRAU FAHRENKOPF *rushes back to her family. They talk excitedly in German about the iguana.*]

SHANNON: If you mean Mexican chicken, that's no recommendation. Mexican chickens are scavengers and they taste like what they scavenge.

MAXINE: Naw, I mean Texas chicken.

SHANNON [*dreamily*]: Texas . . . chicken. . . .

[*He paces restlessly down the verandah.* MAXINE *divides her attention between his tall, lean figure, that seems incapable of stillness, and the wriggling bodies of the Mexican boys lying on their stomachs half under the verandah—as if she were mentally comparing two opposite attractions to her simple, sensual nature.* SHANNON *turns at the end of the verandah and sees her eyes fixed on him.*]

SHANNON: What is the sex of this iguana, Maxine?

MAXINE: Hah, who cares about the sex of an iguana . . . [*He passes close by her.*] . . . except another . . . iguana?

SHANNON: Haven't you heard the limerick about iguanas? [*He removes her drink from her hand and it seems as if he might drink it, but he only sniffs it, with an expression of repugnance. She chuckles.*]

> There was a young gaucho named Bruno
> Who said about love, This I do know:
> Women are fine, and sheep are divine,
> But iguanas are—*Número Uno!*

[*On* "Número Uno" SHANNON *empties* MAXINE'S *drink over the railing, deliberately onto the humped, wriggling posterior of* PEDRO, *who springs up with angry protests.*]

PEDRO: Me cago . . . hijo de la . . .

MAXINE: Shannon! Hah! My spies told me that you were back under the border! . . . [that] you went through Saltillo last week with a busload of women—a whole busload of females, all females, hah!

SHANNON: For God's sake, help me with her.
MAXINE: You know I'll help you, baby, but why don't you lay
off the young ones and **cultivate** an interest in normal
grown-up women?

HANNAH:
Is this the Costa
Verde Hotel?

MISS FELLOWES:
I've taken a look at those
rooms and they'd make
a room at the "Y" look
like a suite at the Ritz.

CHARLOTTE: Larry, open this door and let me in! I know you're in there, Larry!

CHARLOTTE: I don't believe you don't love me.

SHANNON: Honey, it's almost impossible for anybody to believe they're not loved by someone they believe they love, but, honey, I love *nobody*.

SHANNON:
You're going to get me
kicked out of Blake Tours,
Charlotte.

HANNAH:
Isn't that lovely gold cross enough to convince the ladies?

SHANNON:
No, they know I redeemed it from a Mexico City pawnshop, and they suspect that that's where I got it in the first place.

SHANNON: I shouted after them, go on, go home and close your house windows, all your windows and doors, against the truth about God!

MAXINE: I want you to lay off him, honey. You're not for Shannon and Shannon isn't for you.

HANNAH: Mrs. Faulk, I'm a New England spinster who is pushing forty.

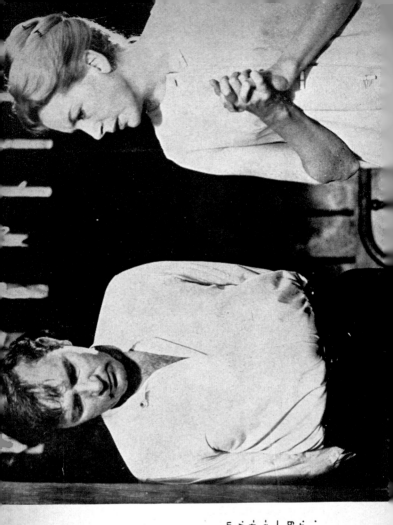

SHANNON:
I think I first *faced* it in that nameless country. The gradual, rapid, natural, unnatural—predestined, accidental — cracking up and going to pieces of young Mr. T. Lawrence Shannon . . .

SHANNON: Qué? Qué?

MAXINE: Vete!

[SHANNON *laughs viciously. The iguana escapes and both boys rush shouting after it. One of them dives on it and recaptures it at the edge of the jungle.*]

PANCHO: La iguana se escapó.

MAXINE: Cójela, cójela! La cojiste? Si no la cojes, te morderá el culo. La cojiste?

PEDRO: La cojí.*

[*The boys wriggle back under the verandah with the iguana.*]

MAXINE [*returning to* SHANNON]: I thought you were gonna break down and take a drink, Reverend.

SHANNON: Just the odor of liquor makes me feel nauseated.

MAXINE: You couldn't smell it if you got it *in* you. [*She touches his sweating forehead. He brushes her hand off like an insect.*] Hah! [*She crosses over to the liquor cart, and he looks after her with a sadistic grin.*]

SHANNON: Maxine honey, whoever told you that you look good in tight pants was not a sincere friend of yours.

[*He turns away. At the same instant, a crash and a hoarse, startled outcry are heard from* NONNO'S *cubicle.*]

MAXINE: I knew it, I *knew* it! The old man's took a fall!

[SHANNON *rushes into the cubicle, followed by* MAXINE.]

[*The light has been gradually, steadily dimming during the incident of the iguana's escape. There is, in effect, a division*

---

* The iguana's escaped. / Get it, get it! Have you got it? If you don't, it'll bite your behind. Have you got it? / He's got it.

of scenes here, though it is accomplished without a black-out or curtain. As SHANNON *and* MAXINE *enter* NONNO'S *cubicle,* HERR FAHRENKOPF *appears on the now twilit verandah. He turns on an outsize light fixture that is suspended from overhead, a full pearly-moon of a light globe that gives an unearthly luster to the scene. The great pearly globe is decorated by night insects, large but gossamer moths that have immolated themselves on its surface: the light through their wings gives them an opalescent color, a touch of fantasy.*

[*Now* SHANNON *leads the old poet out of his cubicle, onto the facing verandah. The old man is impeccably dressed in snow-white linen with a black string tie. His leonine mane of hair gleams like silver as he passes under the globe.*]

NONNO: No bones broke, I'm made out of India rubber!

SHANNON: A traveler-born falls down many times in his travels.

NONNO: Hannah? [*His vision and other senses have so far deteriorated that he thinks he is being led out by* HANNAH.] I'm pretty sure I'm going to finish it here.

SHANNON [*shouting, gently*]: I've got the same feeling, Grampa.

[MAXINE *follows them out of the cubicle.*]

NONNO: I've never been surer of anything in my life.

SHANNON [*gently and wryly*]: I've never been surer of anything in mine either.

[HERR FAHRENKOPF *has been listening with an expression of entrancement to his portable radio, held close to his ear, the sound unrealistically low. Now he turns it off and makes an excited speech.*]

HERR FAHRENKOPF: The London fires have spread all the way from the heart of London to the Channel coast! Goering,

Field Marshall Goering, calls it "the new phase of conquest!"
Superfirebombs! Each night!

[NONNO *catches only the excited tone of this announcement
and interprets it as a request for a recitation. He strikes the
floor with his cane, throws back his silver-maned head and
begins the delivery in a grand, declamatory style.*]

NONNO:
  Youth must be wanton, youth must be quick,
  Dance to the candle while lasteth the wick,

  Youth must be foolish and. . . .

[NONNO *falters on the line, a look of confusion and fear on
his face. The Germans are amused.* WOLFGANG *goes up to*
NONNO *and shouts into his face.*]

WOLFGANG: Sir? What is your age? How old?

[HANNAH, *who has just returned to the verandah, rushes up
to her grandfather and answers for him.*]

HANNAH: He is ninety-seven years *young!*

HERR FAHRENKOPF: How old?

HANNAH: Ninety-seven—almost a *century young!*

[HERR FAHRENKOPF *repeats this information to his beaming
wife and* HILDA *in German.*]

NONNO [*cutting in on the Germans*]:
  Youth must be foolish and mirthful and blind,
  Gaze not before and glance not behind,

  Mark not. . . .

[*He falters again.*]

HANNAH [*prompting him, holding tightly onto his arm*]:
  Mark not the shadow that darkens the way—

[*They recite the next lines together.*]
Regret not the glitter of any lost day,

But laugh with no reason except the red wine,
For youth must be youthful and foolish and blind!

[*The Germans are loudly amused.* WOLFGANG *applauds directly in the old poet's face.* NONNO *makes a little unsteady bow, leaning forward precariously on his cane.* SHANNON *takes a firm hold of his arm as* HANNAH *turns to the Germans, opening her portfolio of sketches and addressing* WOLFGANG.]

HANNAH: Am I right in thinking you are on your honeymoon? [*There is no response, and she repeats the question in German while* FRAU FAHRENKOPF *laughs and nods vehemently*.] Habe ich recht das Sie auf Ihrer Hochzeitsreise sind? Was für eine hübsche junge Braut! Ich mache Pastell-Skizzen . . . darf ich, würden Sie mir erlauben . . . ? Würden Sie, bitte . . . bitte. . . .

[HERR FAHRENKOPF *bursts into a Nazi marching song and leads his party to the champagne bucket on the table at the left.* SHANNON *has steered* NONNO *to the other table.*]

NONNO [*exhilarated*]: Hannah! What was the *take?*

HANNAH [*embarrassed*]: Grandfather, sit down, please stop shouting!

NONNO: Hah? Did they cross your palm with silver or paper, Hannah?

HANNAH [*almost desperately*]: Nonno! No more shouting! Sit down at the table. It's time to *eat!*

SHANNON: Chow time, Grampa.

NONNO [*confused but still shouting*]: How much did they come across with?

HANNAH: Nonno! *Please!*

NONNO: Did they, did you . . . sell 'em a . . . water color?

HANNAH: No sale, Grandfather!

MAXINE: Hah!

[HANNAH *turns to* SHANNON, *her usual composure shattered, or nearly so.*]

HANNAH: He won't sit down or stop shouting.

NONNO [*blinking and beaming with the grotesque suggestion of an old coquette*]: Hah? How rich did we strike it, Hannah?

SHANNON: *You* sit down, Miss Jelkes. [*He says it with gentle authority, to which she yields. He takes hold of the old man's forearm and places in his hand a crumpled Mexican bill.*] Sir? Sir? [*He is shouting.*] Five! Dollars! I'm putting it in your pocket.

HANNAH: We can't accept . . . gratuities, Mr. Shannon.

SHANNON: Hell, I gave him five pesos.

NONNO: Mighty good for one poem!

SHANNON: Sir? Sir? The *pecuniary rewards* of a *poem* are *grossly inferior* to its *merits*, always!

[*He is being fiercely, almost mockingly tender with the old man—a thing we are when the pathos of the old, the ancient, the dying is such a wound to our own (savagely beleaguered) nerves and sensibilities that this outside demand on us is beyond our collateral, our emotional reserve. This is as true of* HANNAH *as it is of* SHANNON, *of course. They have both overdrawn their reserves at this point of the encounter between them.*]

NONNO: Hah? Yes. . . . [*He is worn out now, but still shouting.*] We're going to clean up in this place!

SHANNON: You bet you're going to clean up here!

[MAXINE *utters her one-note bark of a laugh.* SHANNON *throws a hard roll at her. She wanders amiably back toward the German table.*]

NONNO [*tottering, panting, hanging onto* SHANNON'S *arm, thinking it is* HANNAH'S]: Is the, the . . . dining room . . . crowded? [*He looks blindly about with wild surmise.*]

SHANNON: Yep, it's filled to capacity! There's a big crowd at the door! [*His voice doesn't penetrate the old man's deafness.*]

NONNO: If there's a cocktail lounge, Hannah, we ought to . . . work that . . . first. Strike while the iron is hot, ho, ho, while it's hot. . . . [*This is like a delirium—only as strong a woman as* HANNAH *could remain outwardly impassive.*]

HANNAH: He thinks you're me, Mr. Shannon. Help him into a chair. Please stay with him a minute, I. . . .

[*She moves away from the table and breathes as if she has just been dragged up half-drowned from the sea.* SHANNON *eases the old man into a chair. Almost at once* NONNO'S *feverish vitality collapses and he starts drifting back toward half sleep.*]

SHANNON [*crossing to* HANNAH]: What're you breathing like that for?

HANNAH: Some people take a drink, some take a pill. I just take a few deep breaths.

SHANNON: You're making too much out of this. It's a natural thing in a man as old as Grampa.

HANNAH: I know, I know. He's had more than one of these little "cerebral accidents" as you call them, and all in the last few months. He was amazing till lately. I had to show his passport to prove that he was the oldest living and practicing poet on earth. We did well, we made expenses and *more!* But . . . when I saw he was failing, I tried to persuade him to go back to Nantucket, but he conducts our tours. He said, "No, *Mexico!*" So here we are on this windy hilltop like a pair of

scarecrows. . . . The bus from Mexico City broke down at an
altitude of 15,000 feet above sea level. That's when I think the
latest cerebral incident happened. It isn't so much the loss of
hearing and sight but the . . . dimming out of the mind that I
can't bear, because until lately, just lately, his mind was amaz-
ingly clear. But yesterday? In Taxco? I spent nearly all we had
left on the wheelchair for him and still he insisted that we go on
with the trip till we got to the sea, the . . . cradle of life as he
calls it. . . . [*She suddenly notices* NONNO, *sunk in his chair as
if lifeless. She draws a sharp breath, and goes quietly to him.*]

SHANNON [*to the Mexican boys*]: Servicio! Aquí! [*The force
of his order proves effective: they serve the fish course.*]

HANNAH: What a kind man you are. I don't know how to
thank you, Mr. Shannon. I'm going to wake him up now.
Nonno! [*She claps her hands quietly at his ear. The old man
rouses with a confused, breathless chuckle.*] Nonno, linen
napkins. [*She removes a napkin from the pocket of her smock.*]
I always carry one with me, you see, in case we run into paper
napkins as sometimes happens, you see. . . .

NONNO: Wonderful place here. . . . I hope it is à la carte,
Hannah, I want a very light supper so I won't get sleepy. I'm
going to work after supper. I'm going to finish it here.

HANNAH: Nonno? We've made a friend here. Nonno, this is
the Reverend Mr. Shannon.

NONNO [*struggling out of his confusion*]: Reverend?

HANNAH [*shouting to him*]: Mr. Shannon's an Episcopal
clergyman, Nonno.

NONNO: A man of God?

HANNAH: A man of God, on vacation.

NONNO: Hannah, tell him I'm too old to baptize and too
young to bury but on the market for marriage to a rich widow,
fat, fair and forty.

[NONNO *is delighted by all of his own little jokes. One can see him exchanging these pleasantries with the rocking-chair brigades of summer hotels at the turn of the century—and with professors' wives at little colleges in New England. But now it has become somewhat grotesque in a touching way, this desire to please, this playful manner, these venerable jokes.* SHANNON *goes along with it. The old man touches something in him which is outside of his concern with himself. This part of the scene, which is played in a "scherzo" mood, has an accompanying windy obligato on the hilltop— all through it we hear the wind from the sea gradually rising, sweeping up the hill through the rain forest, and there are fitful glimmers of lightning in the sky.*]

NONNO: But very few ladies ever go past forty if you believe 'em, ho, ho! Ask him to . . . give the blessing. Mexican food needs blessing.

SHANNON: Sir, you give the blessing. I'll be right with you. [*He has broken one of his shoelaces.*]

NONNO: Tell him I will oblige him on one condition.

SHANNON: What condition, sir?

NONNO: That you'll keep my daughter company when I retire after dinner. I go to bed with the chickens and get up with the roosters, ho, ho! So you're a man of God. A benedict or a bachelor?

SHANNON: Bachelor, sir. No sane and civilized woman would have me, Mr. Coffin.

NONNO: What did he say, Hannah?

HANNAH [*embarrassed*]: Nonno, give the blessing.

NONNO [*not hearing this*]: I call her my daughter, but she's my daughter's daughter. We've been in charge of each other since she lost both her parents in the very first automobile crash on the island of Nantucket.

HANNAH: Nonno, give the blessing.

NONNO: She isn't a modern flapper, she isn't modern and she—doesn't flap, but she was brought up to be a wonderful wife and mother. But . . . I'm a selfish old man so I've kept her all to myself.

HANNAH [*shouting into his ear*]: Nonno, Nonno, the blessing!

NONNO [*rising with an effort*]: Yes, the blessing. Bless this food to our use, and ourselves to Thy service. Amen. [*He totters back into his chair.*]

SHANNON: Amen.

[NONNO'S *mind starts drifting, his head drooping forward. He murmurs to himself.*]

SHANNON: How good is the old man's poetry?

HANNAH: My grandfather was a fairly well-known minor poet before the First World War and for a little while after.

SHANNON: In the minor league, huh?

HANNAH: Yes, a minor league poet with a major league spirit. I'm proud to be his granddaughter. . . . [*She draws a pack of cigarettes from her pocket, then replaces it immediately without taking a cigarette.*]

NONNO [*very confused*]: Hannah, it's too hot for . . . hot cereals this . . . morning. . . . [*He shakes his head several times with a rueful chuckle.*]

HANNAH: He's not quite back, you see, he thinks it's morning. [*She says this as if making an embarrassing admission, with a quick, frightened smile at* SHANNON.]

SHANNON: Fantastic—*fantastic*.

HANNAH: That word "fantastic" seems to be your favorite word, Mr. Shannon.

SHANNON [*looking out gloomily from the verandah*]: Yeah, well, you know we—live on two levels, Miss Jelkes, the realistic level and the fantastic level, and which is the real one, really. . . .

HANNAH: I would say both, Mr. Shannon.

SHANNON: But when you live on the fantastic level as I have lately but have got to operate on the realistic level, that's when you're spooked, that's the spook. . . . [*This is said as if it were a private reflection.*] I thought I'd shake the spook here but conditions have changed here. I didn't know the patrona had turned to a widow, a sort of bright widow spider. [*He chuckles almost like* NONNO.]

[MAXINE *has pushed one of those gay little brass-and-glass liquor carts around the corner of the verandah. It is laden with an ice bucket, coconuts and a variety of liquors. She hums gaily to herself as she pushes the cart close to the table.*]

MAXINE: Cocktails, anybody?

HANNAH: No, thank you, Mrs. Faulk, I don't think we care for any.

SHANNON: People don't drink cocktails between the fish and the entrée, Maxine honey.

MAXINE: Grampa needs a toddy to wake him up. Old folks need a toddy to pick 'em up. [*She shouts into the old man's ear.*] Grampa! How about a toddy? [*Her hips are thrust out at* SHANNON.]

SHANNON: Maxine, your ass—excuse me, Miss Jelkes—your hips, Maxine, are too fat for this verandah.

MAXINE: Hah! Mexicans like 'em, if I can judge by the pokes and pinches I get in the busses to town. And so do the Germans. Ev'ry time I go near Herr Fahrenkopf he gives me a pinch or a goose.

SHANNON: Then go near him again for another goose.

MAXINE: Hah! I'm mixing Grampa a Manhattan with two cherries in it so he'll live through dinner.

SHANNON: Go on back to your Nazis, I'll mix the Manhattan for him. [*He goes to the liquor cart.*]

MAXINE [*to* HANNAH]: How about you, honey, a little soda with lime juice?

HANNAH: Nothing for me, thank you.

SHANNON: Don't make nervous people more nervous, Maxine.

MAXINE: You better let me mix that toddy for Grampa, you're making a mess of it, Shannon.

[*With a snort of fury, he thrusts the liquor cart like a battering ram at her belly. Some of the bottles fall off it; she thrusts it right back at him.*]

HANNAH: Mrs. Faulk, Mr. Shannon, this is childish, please stop it!

[*The Germans are attracted by the disturbance. They cluster around, laughing delightedly.* SHANNON *and* MAXINE *seize opposite ends of the rolling liquor cart and thrust it toward each other, both grinning fiercely as gladiators in mortal combat. The Germans shriek with laughter and chatter in German.*]

HANNAH: Mr. Shannon, stop it! [*She appeals to the Germans.*] *Bitte!* Nehmen Sie die Spirituosen weg. Bitte, nehmen Sie die weg.

[SHANNON *has wrested the cart from* MAXINE *and pushed it at the Germans. They scream delightedly. The cart crashes into the wall of the verandah.* SHANNON *leaps down the steps and runs into the foliage. Birds scream in the rain forest. Then sudden quiet returns to the verandah as the Germans go back to their own table.*]

MAXINE: Crazy, black Irish Protestant son of a . . . Protestant!

HANNAH: Mrs. Faulk, he's putting up a struggle not to drink.

MAXINE: Don't interfere. You're an interfering woman.

HANNAH: Mr. Shannon is dangerously . . . disturbed.

MAXINE: I know how to handle him, honey—you just met him today. Here's Grampa's Manhattan cocktail with two cherries in it.

HANNAH: Please don't call him Grampa.

MAXINE: Shannon calls him Grampa.

HANNAH [*taking the drink*]: He doesn't make it sound condescending, but you *do*. My grandfather is a gentleman in the true sense of the word, he is a *gentle man*.

MAXINE: What are you?

HANNAH: I am his granddaughter.

MAXINE: Is that all you are?

HANNAH: I think it's enough to be.

MAXINE: Yeah, but you're also a deadbeat, using that dying old man for a front to get in places without the cash to pay even one day in advance. Why, you're dragging him around with you like Mexican beggars carry around a sick baby to put the touch on the tourists.

HANNAH: I told you I had no money.

MAXINE: Yes, and I told you that I was a widow—recent. In such a financial hole they might as well have buried me with my husband.

[SHANNON *reappears from the jungle foliage but remains unnoticed by* HANNAH *and* MAXINE.]

HANNAH [*with forced calm*]: Tomorrow morning, at daybreak, I will go in town. I will set up my easel in the plaza and peddle my water colors and sketch tourists. I am not a weak person, my failure here isn't typical of me.

MAXINE: I'm not a weak person either.

HANNAH: No. By no means, no. Your strength is awe-inspiring.

MAXINE: You're goddam right about that, but how do you think you'll get to Acapulco without the cabfare or even the busfare there?

HANNAH: I will go on shanks' mare, Mrs. Faulk—islanders are good walkers. And if you doubt my word for it, if you really think I came here as a deadbeat, then I will put my grandfather back in his wheelchair and push him back down this hill to the road and all the way back into town.

MAXINE: Ten miles, with a storm coming up?

HANNAH: Yes, I would—I will. [*She is dominating* MAXINE *in this exchange. Both stand beside the table.* NONNO'S *head is drooping back into sleep.*]

MAXINE: I wouldn't let you.

HANNAH: But you've made it clear that you don't want us to stay here for one night even.

MAXINE: The storm would blow that old man out of his wheelchair like a dead leaf.

HANNAH: He would prefer that to staying where he's not welcome, and I would prefer it for him, and for myself, Mrs. Faulk. [*She turns to the Mexican boys.*] Where is his wheelchair? Where is my grandfather's wheelchair?

[*This exchange has roused the old man. He struggles up from his chair, confused, strikes the floor with his cane and starts declaiming a poem.*]

NONNO:

> Love's an old remembered song
> A drunken fiddler plays,
> Stumbling crazily along
> Crooked alleyways.
> When his heart is mad with music
> He will play the—

HANNAH: Nonno, not now, Nonno! He thought someone asked for a poem. [*She gets him back into the chair.* HANNAH *and* MAXINE *are still unaware of* SHANNON.]

MAXINE: Calm down, honey.

HANNAH: I'm perfectly calm, Mrs. Faulk.

MAXINE: I'm *not.* That's the trouble.

HANNAH: I understand that, Mrs. Faulk. You lost your husband just lately. I think you probably miss him more than you know.

MAXINE: No, the trouble is Shannon.

HANNAH: You mean his nervous state and his . . . ?

MAXINE: No, I just mean Shannon. I want you to lay off him, honey. You're not for Shannon and Shannon isn't for you.

HANNAH: Mrs. Faulk, I'm a New England spinster who is pushing forty.

MAXINE: I got the vibrations between you—I'm very good at catching vibrations between people—and there sure was a vibration between you and Shannon the moment you got here. That, just that, believe me, nothing but that has made this . . . misunderstanding between us. So if you just don't mess with Shannon, you and your Grampa can stay on here as long as you want to, honey.

HANNAH: Oh, Mrs. Faulk, do I look like a *vamp?*

MAXINE: They come in all types. I've had all types of them here.

[SHANNON *comes over to the table.*]

SHANNON: Maxine, I told you don't make nervous people more nervous, but you wouldn't listen.

MAXINE: What you need is a drink.

SHANNON: Let me decide about that.

HANNAH: Won't you sit down with us, Mr. Shannon, and eat something? Please. You'll feel better.

SHANNON: I'm not hungry right now.

HANNAH: Well, just sit down with us, won't you?

[SHANNON *sits down with* HANNAH.]

MAXINE [*warningly to* HANNAH]: O.K. O.K. . . .

NONNO [*rousing a bit and mumbling*]: Wonderful . . . wonderful place here.

[MAXINE *retires from the table and wheels the liquor cart over to the German party.*]

SHANNON: Would you have gone through with it?

HANNAH: Haven't you ever played poker, Mr. Shannon?

SHANNON: You mean you were bluffing?

HANNAH: Let's say I was drawing to an inside straight. [*The wind rises and sweeps up the hill like a great waking sigh from the ocean.*] It *is* going to storm. I hope your ladies aren't still out in that, that . . . glass-bottomed boat, observing the, uh, submarine . . . marvels.

SHANNON: That's because you don't know these ladies. How-

ever, they're back from the boat trip. They're down at the
cantina, dancing together to the jukebox and hatching new plots
to get me kicked out of Blake Tours.

HANNAH: What would you do if you. . . .

SHANNON: Got the sack? Go back to the Church or take the
long swim to China. [HANNAH *removes a crumpled pack of
cigarettes from her pocket. She discovers only two left in the
pack and decides to save them for later. She returns the pack
to her pocket.*] May I have one of your cigarettes, Miss Jelkes?
[*She offers him the pack. He takes it from her and crumples it
and throws it off the verandah.*] Never smoke those, they're
made out of tobacco from cigarette stubs that beggars pick up
off sidewalks and out of gutters in Mexico City. [*He produces
a tin of English cigarettes.*] Have these—Benson and Hedges,
imported, in an airtight tin, my luxury in my life.

HANNAH: Why—thank you, I will, since you have thrown
mine away.

SHANNON: I'm going to tell you something about yourself.
You are a lady, a *real* one and a *great* one.

HANNAH: What have I done to merit that compliment from
you?

SHANNON: It isn't a compliment, it's just a report on what
I've noticed about you at a time when it's hard for me to notice
anything outside myself. You took out those Mexican cigarettes,
you found you just had two left, you can't afford to buy a new
pack of even that cheap brand, so you put them away for later.
Right?

HANNAH: Mercilessly accurate, Mr. Shannon.

SHANNON: But when I asked you for one, you offered it to
me without a sign of reluctance.

HANNAH: Aren't you making a big point out of a small
matter?

SHANNON: Just the opposite, honey, I'm making a small point out of a very large matter. [SHANNON *has put a cigarette in his lips but has no matches.* HANNAH *has some and she lights his cigarette for him.*] How'd you learn how to light a match in the wind?

HANNAH: Oh, I've learned lots of useful little things like that. I wish I'd learned some *big* ones.

SHANNON: Such as what?

HANNAH: How to help you, Mr. Shannon. . . .

SHANNON: Now I know why I came here!

HANNAH: To meet someone who can light a match in the wind?

SHANNON [*looking down at the table, his voice choking*]: To meet someone who wants to *help* me, Miss Jelkes. . . . [*He makes a quick, embarrassed turn in the chair, as if to avoid her seeing that he has tears in his eyes. She regards him steadily and tenderly, as she would her grandfather.*]

HANNAH: Has it been so long since anyone has wanted to help you, or have you just. . . .

SHANNON: Have I—what?

HANNAH: Just been so much involved with a struggle in your-self that you haven't noticed when people have wanted to help you, the little they can? I know people torture each other many times like devils, but sometimes they do see and know each other, you know, and then, if they're decent, they do want to help each other all that they can. Now will you please help *me*? Take care of Nonno while I remove my water colors from the annex verandah because the storm is coming up by leaps and bounds now.

[*He gives a quick, jerky nod, dropping his face briefly into the cup of his hands. She murmurs* "Thank you" *and springs up, starting along the verandah. Halfway across, as the storm*

*closes in upon the hilltop with a thunderclap and a sound of
rain coming,* HANNAH *turns to look back at the table.*
SHANNON *has risen and gone around the table to* NONNO.]

SHANNON: Grampa? Nonno? Let's get up before the rain hits
us, Grampa.

NONNO: What? What?

[SHANNON *gets the old man out of his chair and shepherds
him to the back of the verandah as* HANNAH *rushes toward
the annex. The Mexican boys hastily clear the table, fold it
up and lean it against the wall.* SHANNON *and* NONNO *turn
and face toward the storm, like brave men facing a firing
squad.* MAXINE *is excitedly giving orders to the boys.*]

MAXINE: Pronto, pronto, muchachos! Pronto, pronto!*
Llevaros todas las cosas! Pronto, pronto! Recoje los platos!
Apúrate con el mantel!

PEDRO: Nos estamos dando prisa!

PANCHO: Que el chubasco lave los platos!

[*The German party look on the storm as a Wagnerian climax.
They rise from their table as the boys come to clear it, and
start singing exultantly. The storm, with its white convulsions
of light, is like a giant white bird attacking the hilltop of the
Costa Verde.* HANNAH *reappears with her water colors
clutched against her chest.*]

SHANNON: Got them?

HANNAH: Yes, just in time. Here is your God, Mr. Shannon.

SHANNON [*quietly*]: Yes, I see him, I hear him, I know him.
And if he doesn't know that I know him, let him strike me
dead with a bolt of his lightning.

---

* Hurry, hurry, boys! Pick everything up! Get the plates! Hurry
with the table cloth! / We *are* hurrying! / Let the storm wash the
plates!

[*He moves away from the wall to the edge of the verandah as a fine silver sheet of rain descends off the sloping roof, catching the light and dimming the figures behind it. Now everything is silver, delicately lustrous.* SHANNON *extends his hands under the rainfall, turning them in it as if to cool them. Then he cups them to catch the water in his palms and bathes his forehead with it. The rainfall increases. The sound of the marimba band at the beach cantina is brought up the hill by the wind.* SHANNON *lowers his hands from his burning forehead and stretches them out through the rain's silver sheet as if he were reaching for something outside and beyond himself. Then nothing is visible but these reaching-out hands. A pure white flash of lightning reveals* HANNAH *and* NONNO *against the wall, behind* SHANNON, *and the electric globe suspended from the roof goes out, the power extinguished by the storm. A clear shaft of light stays on* SHANNON'S *reaching-out hands till the stage curtain has fallen, slowly.*]*

INTERMISSION

---

* *Note:* In staging, the plastic elements should be restrained so that they don't take precedence over the more important human values. It should not seem like an "effect curtain." The faint, windy music of the marimba band from the cantina should continue as the house-lights are brought up for the intermission.

Act Three

The verandah, several hours later. Cubicles number 3, 4, and 5 are dimly lighted within. We see HANNAH *in number 3, and* NONNO *in number 4.* SHANNON, *who has taken off his shirt, is seated at a table on the verandah, writing a letter to his Bishop. All but this table have been folded and stacked against the wall and* MAXINE *is putting the hammock back up which had been taken down for dinner. The electric power is still off and the cubicles are lighted by oil lamps. The sky has cleared completely, the moon is making for full and it bathes the scene in an almost garish silver which is intensified by the wetness from the recent rainstorm. Everything is drenched—there are pools of silver here and there on the floor of the verandah. At one side a smudge-pot is burning to repel the mosquitoes, which are particularly vicious after a tropical downpour when the wind is exhausted.*

SHANNON *is working feverishly on the letter to the Bishop, now and then slapping at a mosquito on his bare torso. He is shiny with perspiration, still breathing like a spent runner, muttering to himself as he writes and sometimes suddenly drawing a loud deep breath and simultaneously throwing back his head to stare up wildly at the night sky.* HANNAH *is seated on a straight-back chair behind the mosquito netting in her cubicle— very straight herself, holding a small book in her hands but looking steadily over it at* SHANNON, *like a guardian angel. Her hair has been let down.* NONNO *can be seen in his cubicle rocking back and forth on the edge of the narrow bed as he goes over and over the lines of his first new poem in "twenty-some years"—which he knows is his last one.*

Now and then the sound of distant music drifts up from the beach cantina.

MAXINE: Workin' on your sermon for next Sunday, Rev'-rend?

SHANNON: I'm writing a very important letter, Maxine. [*He means don't disturb me.*]

MAXINE: Who to, Shannon?

SHANNON: The Dean of the Divinity School at Sewanee. [MAXINE *repeats* "Sewanee" *to herself, tolerantly.*] Yes, and I'd appreciate it very much, Maxine honey, if you'd get Pedro or Pancho to drive into town with it tonight so it will go out first thing in the morning.

MAXINE: The kids took off in the station wagon already—for some cold beers and hot whores at the cantina.

SHANNON: "Fred's dead"—he's lucky. . . .

MAXINE: Don't misunderstand me about Fred, baby. I miss him, but we'd not only stopped sleeping together, we'd stopped talking together except in grunts—no quarrels, no misunderstandings, but if we exchanged two grunts in the course of a day, it was a long conversation we'd had that day between us.

SHANNON: Fred knew when I was spooked—wouldn't have to tell him. He'd just look at me and say, "Well, Shannon, you're spooked."

MAXINE: Yeah, well, Fred and me'd reached the point of just grunting.

SHANNON: Maybe he thought you'd turned into a pig, Maxine.

MAXINE: Hah! You know damn well that Fred respected me, Shannon, like I did Fred. We just, well, you know . . . age difference. . . .

SHANNON: Well, you've got Pedro and Pancho.

MAXINE: Employees. They don't respect me enough. When you let employees get too free with you, personally, they stop respecting you, Shannon. And it's, well, it's . . . humiliating —not to be . . . respected.

SHANNON: Then take more bus trips to town for the Mexican pokes and the pinches, or get Herr Fahrenkopf to "respect" you, honey.

MAXINE: Hah! You kill me. I been thinking lately of selling out here and going back to the States, to Texas, and operating a tourist camp outside some live town like Houston or Dallas, on a highway, and renting out cabins to business executives wanting a comfortable little intimate little place to give a little after-hours dictation to their cute little secretaries that can't type or write shorthand. Complimentary rum-cocos—bathrooms with bidets. I'll introduce the bidet to the States.

SHANNON: Does everything have to wind up on that level with you, Maxine?

MAXINE: Yes and no, baby. I know the difference between loving someone and just sleeping with someone—even I know about that. [*He starts to rise.*] We've both reached a point where we've got to settle for something that works for us in our lives—even if it isn't on the highest kind of level.

SHANNON: I don't want to rot.

MAXINE: You wouldn't. I wouldn't let you! I know your psychological history. I remember one of your conversations on this verandah with Fred. You was explaining to him how your problems first started. You told him that Mama, your Mama, used to send you to bed before you was ready to sleep —so you practiced the little boy's vice, you amused yourself with yourself. And once she caught you at it and whaled your backside with the back side of a hairbrush because she said she had to punish you for it because it made God mad as much as it did Mama, and she had to punish you for it so God wouldn't punish you for it harder than she would.

SHANNON: I was talking to Fred.

MAXINE: Yeah, but I heard it, all of it. You said you loved God and Mama and so you quit it to please them, but it was your secret pleasure and you harbored a secret resentment against Mama and God for making you give it up. And so you got back at God by preaching atheistical sermons and you got back at Mama by starting to lay young girls.

SHANNON: I have never delivered an atheistical sermon, and never would or could when I go back to the Church.

MAXINE: You're not going back to no Church. Did you mention the charge of statutory rape to the Divinity Dean?

SHANNON [*thrusting his chair back so vehemently that it topples over*]: Why don't you *let up* on me? You haven't let up on me since I got here this morning! *Let up on me!* Will you please *let up* on me?

MAXINE [*smiling serenely into his rage.*]: Aw baby. . . .

SHANNON: What do you mean by "aw baby"? What do you want out of me, Maxine honey?

MAXINE: Just to do this. [*She runs her fingers through his hair. He thrusts her hand away.*]

SHANNON: Ah, God. [*Words fail him. He shakes his head with a slight, helpless laugh and goes down the steps from the verandah.*]

MAXINE: The Chinaman in the kitchen says, "No sweat." . . . "No sweat." He says that's all his philosophy. All the Chinese philosophy in three words, "Mei yoo guanchi"— which is Chinese for "No sweat." . . . With your record and a charge of statutory rape hanging over you in Texas, how could you go to a church except to the Holy Rollers with some lively young female rollers and a bushel of hay on the church floor?

SHANNON: I'll drive into town in the bus to post this letter tonight. [*He has started toward the path. There are sounds below. He divides the masking foliage with his hands and looks down the hill.*]

MAXINE [*descending the steps from the verandah*]: Watch out for the spook, he's out there.

SHANNON: My ladies are up to something. They're all down there on the road, around the bus.

MAXINE: They're running out on you, Shannon.

[*She comes up beside him. He draws back and she looks down the hill. The light in number 3 cubicle comes on and HANNAH rises from the little table that she had cleared for letter-writing. She removes her Kabuki robe from a hook and puts it on as an actor puts on a costume in his dressing room. NONNO's cubicle is also lighted dimly. He sits on the edge of his cot, rocking slightly back and forth, uttering an indistinguishable mumble of lines from his poem.*]

MAXINE: Yeah. There's a little fat man down there that looks like Jake Latta to me. Yep, that's Jake, that's Latta. I reckon Blake Tours has sent him here to take over your party, Shannon. [SHANNON *looks out over the jungle and lights a cigarette with jerky fingers.*] Well, let him do it. No sweat! He's coming up here now. Want me to handle it for you?

SHANNON: I'll handle it for myself. You keep out of it, please.

[*He speaks with a desperate composure.* HANNAH *stands just behind the curtain of her cubicle, motionless as a painted figure, during the scene that follows.* JAKE LATTA *comes puffing up the verandah steps, beaming genially.*]

LATTA: Hi there, Larry.

SHANNON: Hello, Jake. [*He folds his letter into an envelope.*] Mrs. Faulk honey, this goes air special.

MAXINE: First you'd better address it.

SHANNON: Oh!

[SHANNON *laughs and snatches the letter back, fumbling in his pocket for an address book, his fingers shaking uncontrollably.* LATTA *winks at* MAXINE. *She smiles tolerantly.*]

LATTA: How's our boy doin', Maxine?

MAXINE: He'd feel better if I could get him to take a drink.

LATTA: Can't you get a drink down him?

MAXINE: Nope, not even a rum-coco.

LATTA: Let's have a rum-coco, Larry.

SHANNON: You have a rum-coco, Jake. I have a party of ladies to take care of. And I've discovered that situations come up in this business that call for cold, sober judgment. How about you? Haven't you ever made that discovery, Jake? What're you doing here? Are you here with a party?

LATTA: I'm here to pick up your party, Larry boy.

SHANNON: That's interesting! On whose authority, Jake?

LATTA: Blake Tours wired me in Cuernavaca to pick up your party here and put them together with mine cause you'd had this little nervous upset of yours and. . . .

SHANNON: Show me the wire! Huh?

LATTA: The bus driver says you took the ignition key to the bus.

SHANNON: That's right. I have the ignition key to the bus and I have this party and neither the bus or the party will pull out of here till I say so.

LATTA: Larry, you're a sick boy. Don't give me trouble.

SHANNON: What jail did they bail you out of, you fat zero?

LATTA: Let's have the bus key, Larry.

SHANNON: Where did they dig you up? You've got no party in Cuernavaca, you haven't been out with a party since 'thirty-seven.

LATTA: Just give me the bus key, Larry.

SHANNON: In a pig's—snout!—like yours!

LATTA: Where is the reverend's bedroom, Mrs. Faulk?

SHANNON: The bus key is in my pocket. [*He slaps his pants pocket fiercely.*] Here, right here, in my pocket! Want it? Try and get it, Fatso!

LATTA: What language for a reverend to use, Mrs. Faulk. . . .

SHANNON [*holding up the key*]: See it? [*He thrusts it back into his pocket.*] Now go back wherever you crawled from. My party of ladies is staying here three more days because several of them are in no condition to travel and neither—neither am I.

LATTA: They're getting in the bus now.

SHANNON: How are you going to start it?

LATTA: Larry, don't make me call the bus driver up here to hold you down while I get that key away from you. You want to see the wire from Blake Tours? Here. [*He produces the wire.*] Read it.

SHANNON: You sent that wire to yourself.

LATTA: From Houston?

SHANNON: You had it sent you from Houston. What's that

prove? Why, Blake Tours was nothing, *nothing!*—till they got me. You think they'd let me go?—Ho, ho! Latta, it's caught up with you, Latta, all the whores and tequila have hit your brain now, Latta. [LATTA *shouts down the hill for the bus driver.*] Don't you realize what I mean to Blake Tours? Haven't you seen the brochure in which they mention, they brag, that special parties are conducted by the Reverend T. Lawrence Shannon, D.D., noted world traveler, lecturer, son of a minister and grandson of a bishop, and the direct descendant of two colonial governors? [MISS FELLOWES *appears at the verandah steps.*] Miss Fellowes has read the brochure, she's memorized the brochure. She knows what it says about me.

MISS FELLOWES [*to* LATTA]: Have you got the bus key?

LATTA: Bus driver's going to get it away from him, lady. [*He lights a cigar with dirty, shaky fingers.*]

SHANNON: Ha-ha-ha-ha-ha! [*His laughter shakes him back against the verandah wall.*]

LATTA: He's gone. [*He touches his forehead.*]

SHANNON: Why, those ladies . . . have had . . . some of them, most of them if not all of them . . . for the first time in their lives the advantage of contact, social contact, with a gentleman born and bred, whom under no other circumstances they could have possibly met . . . let alone be given the chance to insult and accuse and. . . .

MISS FELLOWES: Shannon! The girls are in the bus and we want to go now, so give up that key. Now!

[HANK, *the bus driver, appears at the top of the path, whistling casually: he is not noticed at first.*]

SHANNON: If I didn't have a decent sense of responsibility to these parties I take out, I would gladly turn over your party— because I don't like your party—to this degenerate here, this Jake Latta of the gutter-rat Lattas. Yes, I would—I would surrender the bus key in my pocket, even to Latta, but I am not that irresponsible, no, I'm not, to the parties that I take out, regardless of the party's treatment of me. I still feel responsible for them till I get them back wherever I picked them up. [HANK *comes onto the verandah.*] Hi, Hank. Are you friend or foe?

HANK: Larry, I got to get that ignition key now so we can get moving down there.

SHANNON: Oh! Then *foe!* I'm disappointed, Hank. I thought you were friend, not foe. [HANK *puts a wrestler's armlock on* SHANNON *and* LATTA *removes the bus key from his pocket.* HANNAH *raises a hand to her eyes.*] O.K., O.K., you've got the bus key. By force. I feel exonerated now of all responsibility. Take the bus and the ladies in it and go. Hey, Jake, did you know they had lesbians in Texas—without the dikes the plains of Texas would be engulfed by the Gulf. [*He nods his head violently toward* MISS FELLOWES, *who springs forward and slaps him.*] Thank you, Miss Fellowes. Latta, hold on a minute. I will not be stranded here. I've had unusual expenses on this trip. Right now I don't have my fare back to Houston or even to Mexico City. Now if there's any truth in your statement that Blake Tours have really authorized you to take over my party, then I am sure they have . . . [*He draws a breath, almost gasping.*] . . . I'm sure they must have given you something in the . . . the nature of . . . *severance* pay? Or at least enough to get me back to the States?

LATTA: I got no money for you.

SHANNON: I hate to question your word, but. . . .

LATTA: We'll drive you back to Mexico City. You can sit up front with the driver.

SHANNON: *You* would do that, Latta. *I'd* find it *humiliating.* Now! Give me my severance pay!

LATTA: Blake Tours is having to refund those ladies half the price of the tour. That's your severance pay. And Miss Fellowes tells me you got plenty of money out of this young girl you seduced in. . . .

SHANNON: Miss Fellowes, did you really make such a . . . ?

MISS FELLOWES: When Charlotte returned that night, she'd cashed two traveler's checks.

SHANNON: After I had spent all my own cash.

MISS FELLOWES: On what? Whores in the filthy places you took her through?

SHANNON: Miss Charlotte cashed two ten-dollar traveler's checks because I had spent all the cash I had on me. And I've never had to, I've certainly never desired to, have relations with whores.

MISS FELLOWES: You took her through ghastly places, such as. . . .

SHANNON: I showed her what she wanted me to show her. Ask her! I showed her San Juan de Letran, I showed her Tenampa and some other places not listed in the Blake Tours brochure. I showed her more than the floating gardens at Xochimilco, Maximilian's Palace, and the mad Empress Carlotta's little homesick chapel, Our Lady of Guadalupe, the monument to Juarez, the relics of the Aztec civilization, the sword of Cortez, the headdress of Montezuma. I showed her what she told me she wanted to see. Where is she? Where is Miss . . . oh, down there with the ladies. [*He leans over the rail and shouts down.*] Charlotte! Charlotte! [MISS FELLOWES *seizes his arm and thrusts him away from the verandah rail.*]

MISS FELLOWES: Don't you dare!

SHANNON: Dare what?

MISS FELLOWES: Call her, speak to her, go near her, you, you . . . *filthy!*

[MAXINE *reappears at the corner of the verandah, with the ceremonial rapidity of a cuckoo bursting from a clock to announce the hour. She just stands there with an incongruous grin, her big eyes unblinking, as if they were painted on her round beaming face.* HANNAH *holds a gold-lacquered Japanese fan motionless but open in one hand; the other hand touches the netting at the cubicle door as if she were checking an impulse to rush to* SHANNON'S *defense. Her attitude has the style of a Kabuki dancer's pose.* SHANNON'S *manner becomes courtly again.*]

SHANNON: Oh, all right, I won't. I only wanted her to confirm my story that I took her out that night at her request, not at my . . . suggestion. All that I did was offer my services to her when *she* told *me* she'd like to see things not listed in the brochure, not usually witnessed by ordinary tourists such as. . . .

MISS FELLOWES: Your hotel bedroom? Later? That too? She came back *flea*-bitten!

SHANNON: Oh, now, don't exaggerate, please. Nobody ever got any fleas off Shannon.

MISS FELLOWES: Her clothes had to be fumigated!

SHANNON: I understand your annoyance, but you are going too far when you try to make out that I gave Charlotte fleas. I don't deny that. . . .

MISS FELLOWES: Wait till they get my *report*!

SHANNON: I don't deny that it's possible to get fleabites on a tour of inspection of what lies under the public surface of cities, off the grand boulevards, away from the nightclubs, even away from Diego Rivera's murals, but. . . .

MISS FELLOWES: Oh, preach that in a pulpit, Reverend Shannon *de*-frocked!

SHANNON [*ominously*]: You've said that once too often. [*He seizes her arm.*] This time before witnesses. Miss Jelkes? Miss Jelkes!

[HANNAH *opens the curtain of her cubicle.*]

HANNAH: Yes, Mr. Shannon, what is it?

SHANNON: You heard what this. . . .

MISS FELLOWES: Shannon! Take your hand off my arm!

SHANNON: Miss Jelkes, just tell me, did you hear what she . . . [*His voice stops oddly with a choked sobbing sound. He runs at the wall and pounds it with his fists.*]

MISS FELLOWES: I spent this entire afternoon and over twenty dollars checking up on this impostor, with long-distance phone calls.

HANNAH: Not impostor—you mustn't say things like that.

MISS FELLOWES: You were locked out of your church!— for atheism and seducing of girls!

SHANNON [*turning about*]: In front of God and witnesses, you are lying, lying!

LATTA: Miss Fellowes, I want you to know that Blake Tours was deceived about this character's background and Blake Tours will see that he is blacklisted from now on at every travel agency in the States.

SHANNON: How about Africa, Asia, Australia? The whole world, Latta, God's world, has been the range of my travels. I haven't stuck to the schedules of the brochures and I've always allowed the ones that were willing to see, to *see!*—the underworlds of all places, and if they had hearts to be touched, feelings to feel with, I gave them a priceless chance to feel and be touched. And none will ever forget it, none of them, ever, never! [*The passion of his speech imposes a little stillness.*]

LATTA: Go on, lie back in your hammock, that's all you're good for, Shannon. [*He goes to the top of the path and shouts down the hill.*] O.K., let's get cracking. Get that luggage strapped on top of the bus, we're moving! [*He starts down the hill with* MISS FELLOWES.]

NONNO [*incongruously, from his cubicle*]:

How calmly does the orange branch
Observe the sky begin to blanch. . . .

[SHANNON *sucks in his breath with an abrupt, fierce sound. He rushes off the verandah and down the path toward the road.* HANNAH *calls after him, with a restraining gesture.* MAXINE *appears on the verandah. Then a great commotion commences below the hill, with shrieks of outrage and squeals of shocked laughter.*]

MAXINE [*rushing to the path*]: Shannon! Shannon! Get back up here, get back up here. Pedro, Pancho, traerme a Shannon. Que está haciendo allí? Oh, my God! Stop him, for God's sake, somebody stop him!

[SHANNON *returns, panting and spent. He is followed by* MAXINE.]

MAXINE: Shannon, go in your room and stay there until that party's gone.

SHANNON: Don't give me orders.

MAXINE: You do what I tell you to do or I'll have you re-moved—you know where.

SHANNON: Don't push me, don't pull at me, Maxine.

MAXINE: All right, do as I say.

SHANNON: Shannon obeys only Shannon.

MAXINE: You'll sing a different tune if they put you where they put you in 'thirty-six. Remember 'thirty-six, Shannon?

SHANNON: O.K., Maxine, just . . . let me breathe alone, please. I won't go but I will lie in the . . . hammock.

MAXINE: Go into Fred's room where I can watch you.

SHANNON: Later, Maxine, not yet.

MAXINE: Why do you always come here to crack up, Shannon?

SHANNON: It's the hammock, Maxine, the hammock by the rain forest.

MAXINE: Shannon, go in your room and stay there until I get back. Oh, my God, the money. They haven't paid the mother-grabbin' bill. I got to go back down there and collect their goddam bill before they. . . . Pancho, vigílalo, entiendes? [*She rushes back down the hill, shouting* "Hey! Just a minute down there!"]

SHANNON: What did I do? [*He shakes his head, stunned.*] I don't know what I did.

[HANNAH *opens the screen of her cubicle but doesn't come out. She is softly lighted so that she looks, again, like a medieval sculpture of a saint. Her pale gold hair catches the soft light. She has let it down and still holds the silver-backed brush with which she was brushing it.*]

SHANNON: God almighty, I . . . what did I do? I don't know what I did. [*He turns to the Mexican boys who have come back up the path.*] Qué hice? Qué hice?

[*There is breathless, spasmodic laughter from the boys as* PANCHO *informs him that he pissed on the ladies' luggage.*]

PANCHO: Tú measte en las maletas de las señoras!

[SHANNON *tries to laugh with the boys, while they bend double with amusement.* SHANNON's *laughter dies out in little choked spasms. Down the hill,* MAXINE's *voice is raised in angry altercation with* JAKE LATTA. MISS FELLOWES' *voice is lifted and then there is a general rhubarb to which is added the roar of the bus motor.*]

SHANNON: There go my ladies, ha, ha! There go my . . . [*He turns about to meet* HANNAH's *grave, compassionate gaze. He tries to laugh again. She shakes her head with a slight restraining gesture and drops the curtain so that her softly luminous figure is seen as through a mist.*] . . . ladies, the last of my—ha, ha!—ladies. [*He bends far over the verandah rail, then straightens violently and with an animal outcry begins to pull at the chain suspending the gold cross about his neck.* PANCHO *watches indifferently as the chain cuts the back of* SHANNON's *neck.* HANNAH *rushes out to him.*]

HANNAH: Mr. Shannon, stop that! You're cutting yourself doing that. That isn't necessary, so stop it! [*to* PANCHO] Agárrale las manos! [PANCHO *makes a halfhearted effort to comply, but* SHANNON *kicks at him and goes on with the furious self-laceration.*] Shannon, let me do it, let me take it off you. Can I take it off you? [*He drops his arms. She struggles with the clasp of the chain but her fingers are too shaky to work it.*]

SHANNON: No, no, it won't come off, I'll have to break it off me.

HANNAH: No, no, wait—I've got it. [*She has now removed it.*]

SHANNON: Thanks. Keep it. Goodbye! [*He starts toward the path down to the beach.*]

HANNAH: Where are you going? What are you going to do?

SHANNON: I'm going swimming. I'm going to swim out to China!

HANNAH: No, no, not tonight, Shannon! Tomorrow . . . tomorrow, Shannon!

[*But he divides the trumpet-flowered bushes and passes through them.* HANNAH *rushes after him, screaming for*

"Mrs. Faulk." MAXINE *can be heard shouting for the Mexican boys.*]

MAXINE: Muchachos, cojerlo! Atarlo! Está loco. Traerlo aquí. Catch him, he's crazy. Bring him back and tie him up!

[*In a few moments* SHANNON *is hauled back through the bushes and onto the verandah by* MAXINE *and the boys. They rope him into the hammock. His struggle is probably not much of a real struggle—histrionics mostly. But* HANNAH *stands wringing her hands by the steps as* SHANNON, *gasping for breath, is tied up.*]

HANNAH: The ropes are too tight on his chest!

MAXINE: No, they're not. He's acting, acting. He likes it! I know this black Irish bastard like nobody ever knowed him, so you keep out of it, honey. He cracks up like this so regular that you can set a calendar by it. Every eighteen months he does it, and twice he's done it here and I've had to pay for his medical care. Now I'm going to call in town to get a doctor to come out here and give him a knockout injection, and if he's not better tomorrow he's going into the Casa de Locos again like he did the last time he cracked up on me!

[*There is a moment of silence.*]

SHANNON: Miss Jelkes?

HANNAH: Yes.

SHANNON: Where are you?

HANNAH: I'm right here behind you. Can I do anything for you?

SHANNON: Sit here where I can see you. Don't stop talking. I have to fight this panic.

[*There is a pause. She moves a chair beside his hammock. The Germans troop up from the beach. They are delighted by the drama that* SHANNON *has provided. In their scanty swimsuits they parade onto the verandah and gather about* SHANNON'S *captive figure as if they were looking at a funny animal in a zoo. Their talk is in German except when they speak directly to* SHANNON *or* HANNAH. *Their heavily handsome figures gleam with oily wetness and they keep chuckling lubriciously.*]

HANNAH: Please! Will you be so kind as to leave him alone?

[*They pretend not to understand her.* FRAU FAHRENKOPF *bends over* SHANNON *in his hammock and speaks to him loudly and slowly in English.*]

FRAU FAHRENKOPF: Is this true you make pee-pee all over the suitcases of the ladies from Texas? Hah? Hah? You run down there to the bus and right in front of the ladies you pees all over the luggage of the ladies from Texas?

[HANNAH'S *indignant protest is drowned in the Rabelaisian laughter of the Germans.*]

HERR FAHRENKOPF: Thees is vunderbar, vunderbar! Hah? Thees is a *epic gesture!* Hah? Thees is the way to demonstrate to ladies that you are a American *gentleman!* Hah?

[*He turns to the others and makes a ribald comment. The two women shriek with amusement,* HILDA *falling back into the arms of* WOLFGANG, *who catches her with his hands over her almost nude breasts.*]

HANNAH [*calling out*]: Mrs. Faulk! Mrs. Faulk! [*She rushes to the verandah angle as* MAXINE *appears there.*] Will you please ask these people to leave him alone. They're tormenting him like an animal in a trap.

[*The Germans are already trooping around the verandah, laughing and capering gaily.*]

SHANNON [*suddenly, in a great shout*]: Regression to infantilism, ha, ha, regression to infantilism . . . The infantile protest, ha, ha, ha, the infantile expression of rage at Mama and rage at God and rage at the goddam crib, and rage at the everything, rage at the . . . everything. . . . Regression to infantilism. . . .

[*Now all have left but* HANNAH *and* SHANNON.]

SHANNON: Untie me.

HANNAH: Not yet.

SHANNON: I can't stand being tied up.

HANNAH: You'll have to stand it a while.

SHANNON: It makes me panicky.

HANNAH: I know.

SHANNON: A man can die of panic.

HANNAH: Not if he enjoys it as much as you, Mr. Shannon.

[*She goes into her cubicle directly behind his hammock. The cubicle is lighted and we see her removing a small teapot and a tin of tea from her suitcase on the cot, then a little alcohol burner. She comes back out with these articles.*]

SHANNON: What did you mean by that insulting remark?

HANNAH: What remark, Mr. Shannon?

SHANNON: That I enjoy it.

HANNAH: Oh . . . that.

SHANNON: Yes. That.

HANNAH: That wasn't meant as an insult, just an observation. I don't judge people, I draw them. That's all I do, just draw them, but in order to draw them I have to observe them, don't I?

SHANNON: And you've observed, you think you've observed, that I like being tied in this hammock, trussed up in it like a hog being hauled off to the slaughterhouse, Miss Jelkes.

HANNAH: Who wouldn't like to suffer and atone for the sins of himself and the world if it could be done in a hammock with ropes instead of nails, on a hill that's so much lovelier than Golgotha, the Place of the Skull, Mr. Shannon? There's something almost voluptuous in the way that you twist and groan in that hammock—no nails, no blood, no death. Isn't that a comparatively comfortable, almost voluptuous kind of crucifixion to suffer for the guilt of the world, Mr. Shannon?

[*She strikes a match to light the alcohol burner. A pure blue jet of flame springs up to cast a flickering, rather unearthly glow on their section of the verandah. The glow is delicately refracted by the subtle, faded colors of her robe—a robe given to her by a Kabuki actor who posed for her in Japan.*]

SHANNON: Why have you turned against me all of a sudden, when I need you the most?

HANNAH: I haven't turned against you at all, Mr. Shannon. I'm just attempting to give you a character sketch of yourself, in words instead of pastel crayons or charcoal.

SHANNON: You're certainly suddenly very sure of some New England spinsterish attitudes that I didn't know you had in you. I thought that you were an *emancipated* Puritan, Miss Jelkes.

HANNAH: Who is . . . ever . . . completely?

SHANNON: I thought you were sexless but you've suddenly turned into a woman. Know how I know that? Because you, not me—not me—are taking pleasure in my tied-up condition. All women, whether they face it or not, want to see a man in a tied-up situation. They work at it all their lives, to get a man in a tied-up situation. Their lives are fulfilled, they're satisfied at last, when they get a man, or as many men as they can, in the tied-up situation. [HANNAH *leaves the alcohol burner and teapot and moves to the railing where she grips a verandah post and draws a few deep breaths.*] You don't like this observation of you? The shoe's too tight for comfort when it's on your own foot, Miss Jelkes? Some deep breaths again—feeling panic?

HANNAH [*recovering and returning to the burner*]: I'd like to untie you right now, but let me wait till you've passed through your present disturbance. You're still indulging yourself in your . . . your Passion Play performance. I can't help observing this self-indulgence in you.

SHANNON: What rotten indulgence?

HANNAH: Well, your busload of ladies from the Female College in Texas. I don't like those ladies any more than you do, but after all, they did save up all year to make this Mexican tour, to stay in stuffy hotels and eat the food they're used to. They want to be at home away from home, but you . . . you indulged yourself, Mr. Shannon. You did conduct the tour as if it was just for you, for your own pleasure.

SHANNON: Hell, what pleasure—going through hell all the way?

HANNAH: Yes, but comforted, now and then, weren't you,

by the little musical prodigy under the wing of the college vocal instructor?

SHANNON: Funny, ha-ha funny! Nantucket spinsters have their wry humor, don't they?

HANNAH: Yes, they do. They have to.

SHANNON [*becoming progressively quieter under the cool influence of her voice behind him*]: I can't see what you're up to, Miss Jelkes honey, but I'd almost swear you're making a pot of tea over there.

HANNAH: That is just what I'm doing.

SHANNON: Does this strike you as the right time for a tea party?

HANNAH: This isn't plain tea, this is poppyseed tea.

SHANNON: Are you a slave to the poppy?

HANNAH: It's a mild, sedative drink that helps you get through nights that are hard for you to get through and I'm making it for my grandfather and myself as well as for you, Mr. Shannon. Because, for all three of us, this won't be an easy night to get through. Can't you hear him in his cell number 4, mumbling over and over and over the lines of his new poem? It's like a blind man climbing a staircase that goes to nowhere, that just falls off into space, and I hate to say what it is. . . . [*She draws a few deep breaths behind him.*]

SHANNON: Put some hemlock in his poppyseed tea tonight so he won't wake up tomorrow for the removal to the Casa de Huéspedes. Do that act of mercy. Put in the hemlock and I will consecrate it, turn it to God's blood. Hell, if you'll get me out of his hammock I'll serve it to him myself, I'll be your accomplice in this act of mercy. I'll say, "Take and drink this, the blood of our—"

HANNAH: Stop it! Stop being childishly cruel! I can't stand for a person that I respect to talk and behave like a small, cruel boy, Mr. Shannon.

SHANNON: What've you found to respect in me, Miss . . . Thin-Standing-Up-Female-Buddha?

HANNAH: I respect a person that has had to fight and howl for his decency and his—

SHANNON: *What* decency?

HANNAH: Yes, for his decency and his bit of goodness, much more than I respect the lucky ones that just had theirs handed out to them at birth and never afterwards snatched away from them by . . . unbearable . . . torments, I. . . .

SHANNON: You *respect* me?

HANNAH: I do.

SHANNON: But you just said that I'm taking pleasure in a . . . voluptuous crucifixion without nails. A . . . what? . . . painless atonement for the—

HANNAH [*cutting in*]: Yes, but I think—

SHANNON: Untie me!

HANNAH: Soon, soon. Be patient.

SHANNON: Now!

HANNAH: Not quite yet, Mr. Shannon. Not till I'm reasonably sure that you won't swim out to China, because, you see, I think you think of the . . . "the long swim to China" as another painless atonement. I mean I don't think you think you'd be intercepted by sharks and barracudas before you got far past the barrier reef. And I'm afraid you *would be*. It's as simple as that, if that is simple.

SHANNON: What's simple?

HANNAH: Nothing, except for simpletons, Mr. Shannon.

SHANNON: Do you believe in people being tied up?

HANNAH: Only when they might take the long swim to China.

SHANNON: All right, Miss Thin-Standing-Up-Female-Buddha, just light a Benson & Hedges cigarette for me and put it in my mouth and take it out when you hear me choking on it—if that doesn't seem to you like another bit of voluptuous self-crucifixion.

HANNAH [*looking about the verandah*]: I will, but . . . where did I put them?

SHANNON: I have a pack of my own in my pocket.

HANNAH: Which pocket?

SHANNON: I don't know which pocket, you'll have to frisk me for it. [*She pats his jacket pocket.*]

HANNAH: They're not in your coat pocket.

SHANNON: Then look for them in my pants' pockets.

[*She hesitates to put her hand in his pants' pockets, for a moment.* HANNAH *has always had a sort of fastidiousness, a reluctance, toward intimate physical contact. But after the momentary fastidious hesitation, she puts her hands in his pants' pocket and draws out the cigarette pack.*]

SHANNON: Now light it for me and put it in my mouth.

[*She complies with these directions. Almost at once he chokes and the cigarette is expelled.*]

HANNAH: You've dropped it on you—where is it?

SHANNON [*twisting and lunging about in the hammock*]: It's under me, under me, burning. Untie me, for God's sake, will you—it's burning me through my pants!

HANNAH: Raise your hips so I can—

SHANNON: I can't, the ropes are too tight. Untie me, untieeeee meeeeee!

HANNAH: I've found it, I've got it!

[*But* SHANNON'S *shout has brought* MAXINE *out of her office. She rushes onto the verandah and sits on* SHANNON'S *legs.*]

MAXINE: Now hear this, you crazy black Irish mick, you! You Protestant black Irish looney, I've called up Lopez, Doc Lopez. Remember him—the man in the dirty white jacket that come here the last time you cracked up here? And hauled you off to the Casa de Locos? Where they threw you into that cell with nothing in it but a bucket and straw and a water pipe? That you crawled up the water pipe? And dropped head-down on the floor and got a concussion? Yeah, and I told him you were back here to crack up again and if you didn't quiet down here tonight you should be hauled out in the morning.

SHANNON [*cutting in, with the honking sound of a panicky goose*]: Off, off, off, off, off!

HANNAH: Oh, Mrs. Faulk, Mr. Shannon won't quiet down till he's left alone in the hammock.

MAXINE: Then why don't *you* leave him alone?

HANNAH: I'm not sitting on him and he . . . has to be cared for by someone.

MAXINE: And the someone is *you?*

HANNAH: A long time ago, Mrs. Faulk, I had experience with someone in Mr. Shannon's condition, so I know how necessary it is to let them be quiet for a while.

MAXINE: He wasn't quiet, he was shouting.

HANNAH: He will quiet down again. I'm preparing a sedative tea for him, Mrs. Faulk.

MAXINE: Yeah, I see. Put it out. Nobody cooks here but the Chinaman in the kitchen.

HANNAH: This is just a little alcohol burner, a spirit lamp, Mrs. Faulk.

MAXINE: I know what it is. It goes out! [*She blows out the flame under the burner.*]

SHANNON: Maxine honey? [*He speaks quietly now.*] Stop persecuting this lady. You can't intimidate her. A bitch is no match for a lady except in a brass bed, honey, and sometimes not even there.

[*The Germans are heard shouting for beer—a case of it to take down to the beach.*]

WOLFGANG: Eine Kiste Carta Blanca.

FRAU FAHRENKOPF: Wir haben genug gehabt . . . vielleicht nicht.

HERR FAHRENKOPF: Nein! Niemals genug.

HILDA: Mutter du bist dick . . . aber wir sind es nicht.

SHANNON: Maxine, you're neglecting your duties as a beer-hall waitress. [*His tone is deceptively gentle.*] They want a case of Carta Blanca to carry down to the beach, so give it to 'em . . . and tonight, when the moon's gone down, if you'll let me out of this hammock, I'll try to imagine you as a . . . as a nymph in her teens.

MAXINE: A fat lot of good you'd be in your present condition.

SHANNON: Don't be a sexual snob at your age, honey.

MAXINE: Hah! [*But the unflattering offer has pleased her realistically modest soul, so she goes back to the Germans.*]

SHANNON: Now let me try a bit of your poppyseed tea, Miss Jelkes.

HANNAH: I ran out of sugar, but I had some ginger, some sugared ginger. [*She pours a cup of tea and sips it.*] Oh, it's not well brewed yet, but try to drink some now and the—[*She lights the burner again.*]—the second cup will be better. [*She crouches by the hammock and presses the cup to his lips. He raises his head to sip it, but he gags and chokes.*]

SHANNON: *Caesar's ghost!*—it could be chased by the witches' brew from Macbeth.

HANNAH: Yes, I know, it's still bitter.

[*The Germans appear on the wing of the verandah and go trooping down to the beach, for a beer festival and a moonlight swim. Even in the relative dark they have a luminous color, an almost phosphorescent pink and gold color of skin. They carry with them a case of Carta Blanca beer and the fantastically painted rubber horse. On their faces are smiles of euphoria as they move like a dream-image, starting to sing a marching song as they go.*]

SHANNON: Fiends out of hell with the . . . voices of . . . angels.

HANNAH: Yes, they call it "the logic of contradictions," Mr. Shannon.

SHANNON [*lunging suddenly forward and undoing the loosened ropes*]: Out! Free! Unassisted!

HANNAH: Yes, I never doubted that you could get loose, Mr. Shannon.

SHANNON: Thanks for your help, anyhow.

HANNAH: Where are you going?

[*He has crossed to the liquor cart.*]

SHANNON: Not far. To the liquor cart to make myself a rum-coco.

HANNAH: Oh. . . .

SHANNON [*at the liquor cart*]: Coconut? Check. Machete? Check. Rum? Double check! Ice? The ice bucket's empty. O.K., it's a night for warm drinks. Miss Jelkes? Would you care to have your complimentary rum-coco?

HANNAH: No thank you, Mr. Shannon.

SHANNON: You don't mind me having mine?

HANNAH: Not at all, Mr. Shannon.

SHANNON: You don't disapprove of this weakness, this self-indulgence?

HANNAH: Liquor isn't your problem, Mr. Shannon.

SHANNON: What is my problem, Miss Jelkes?

HANNAH: The oldest one in the world—the need to believe in something or in someone—almost anyone—almost anything . . . something.

SHANNON: Your voice sounds hopeless about it.

HANNAH: No, I'm not hopeless about it. In fact, I've discovered something to believe in.

SHANNON: Something like . . . God?

HANNAH: No.

SHANNON: What?

HANNAH: Broken gates between people so they can reach each other, even if it's just for one night only.

SHANNON: One night stands, huh?

HANNAH: One night . . . communication between them on a

verandah outside their . . . separate cubicles, Mr. Shannon.

SHANNON: You don't mean physically, do you?

HANNAH: No.

SHANNON: I didn't think so. Then what?

HANNAH: A little understanding exchanged between them, a wanting to help each other through nights like this.

SHANNON: Who was the someone you told the widow you'd helped long ago to get through a crack-up like this one I'm going through?

HANNAH: Oh . . . that. Myself.

SHANNON: You?

HANNAH: Yes. I can help you because I've been through what you are going through now. I had something like your spook—I just had a different name for him. I called him the blue devil, and . . . oh . . . we had quite a battle, quite a contest between us.

SHANNON: Which you obviously won.

HANNAH: I couldn't afford to lose.

SHANNON: How'd you beat your blue devil?

HANNAH: I showed him that I could endure him and I made him respect my endurance.

SHANNON: How?

HANNAH: Just by, just by . . . enduring. Endurance is something that spooks and blue devils respect. And they respect all the tricks that panicky people use to outlast and outwit their panic.

SHANNON: Like poppyseed tea?

HANNAH: Poppyseed tea or rum-cocos or just a few deep breaths. Anything, everything, that we take to give them the slip, and so to keep on going.

SHANNON: To where?

HANNAH: To somewhere like this, perhaps. This verandah over the rain forest and the still-water beach, after long, difficult travels. And I don't mean just travels about the world, the earth's surface. I mean . . . subterranean travels, the . . . the journeys that the spooked and bedeviled people are forced to take through the . . . the *unlighted* sides of their natures.

SHANNON: Don't tell me you have a dark side to your nature. [*He says this sardonically*.]

HANNAH: I'm sure I don't have to tell a man as experienced and knowledgeable as you, Mr. Shannon, that everything has its shadowy side?

[*She glances up at him and observes that she doesn't have his attention. He is gazing tensely at something off the verandah. It is the kind of abstraction, not vague but fiercely concentrated, that occurs in madness. She turns to look where he's looking. She closes her eyes for a moment and draws a deep breath, then goes on speaking in a voice like a hypnotist's, as if the words didn't matter, since he is not listening to her so much as to the tone and the cadence of her voice.*]

HANNAH: Everything in the whole solar system has a shadowy side to it except the sun itself—the sun is the single exception. You're not listening, are you?

SHANNON [*as if replying to her*]: The spook is in the rain forest. [*He suddenly hurls his coconut shell with great violence off the verandah, creating a commotion among the jungle birds.*] Good shot—it caught him right on the kisser and his teeth flew out like popcorn from a popper.

HANNAH: Has he gone off—to the dentist?

SHANNON: He's retreated a little way away for a little while, but when I buzz for my breakfast tomorrow, he'll bring it in to me with a grin that'll curdle the milk in the coffee and he'll stink like a . . . a gringo drunk in a Mexican jail who's slept all night in his vomit.

HANNAH: If you wake up before I'm out, I'll bring your coffee in to you . . . if you call me.

SHANNON [*his attention returns to her*]: No, you'll be gone, God help me.

HANNAH: Maybe and maybe not. I might think of something tomorrow to placate the widow.

SHANNON: The widow's implacable, honey.

HANNAH: I think I'll think of something because I have to. I can't let Nonno be moved to the Casa de Huéspedes, Mr. Shannon. Not any more than I could let you take the long swim out to China. You know that. Not if I can prevent it, and when I have to be resourceful, I can be very resourceful.

SHANNON: How'd you get over your crack-up?

HANNAH: I never cracked up, I couldn't afford to. Of course, I nearly did once. I was young once, Mr. Shannon, but I was one of those people who can be young without really having their youth, and not to have your youth when you are young is naturally very disturbing. But I was lucky. My work, this occupational therapy that I gave myself—painting and doing quick character sketches—made me look out of myself, not in, and gradually, at the far end of the tunnel that I was struggling out of I began to see this faint, very faint gray light—the light of the world outside me—and I kept climbing toward it. I had to.

SHANNON: Did it stay a gray light?

HANNAH: No, no, it turned white.

SHANNON: Only white, never gold?

HANNAH: No, it stayed only white, but white is a very good light to see at the end of a long black tunnel you thought would be never-ending, that only God or Death could put a stop to, especially when you . . . since I was . . . far from sure about God.

SHANNON: You're still unsure about him?

HANNAH: Not as unsure as I was. You see, in my profession I have to look hard and close at human faces in order to catch something in them before they get restless and call out, "Waiter, the check, we're leaving." Of course sometimes, a few times, I just see blobs of wet dough that pass for human faces, with bits of jelly for eyes. Then I cue in Nonno to give a recitation, because I can't draw such faces. But those aren't the usual faces, I don't think they're even real. Most times I *do* see something, and I can catch it—I *can*, like I caught something in your face when I sketched you this afternoon with your eyes open. Are you still listening to me? [*He crouches beside her chair, looking up at her intently*.] In Shanghai, Shannon, there is a place that's called the House for the Dying —the old and penniless dying, whose younger, penniless living children and grandchildren take them there for them to get through with their dying on pallets, on straw mats. The first time I went there it shocked me, I ran away from it. But I came back later and I saw that their children and grandchildren and the custodians of the place had put little comforts beside their death-pallets, little flowers and opium candies and religious emblems. That made me able to stay to draw their dying faces. Sometimes only their eyes were still alive, but, Mr. Shannon, those eyes of the penniless dying with those last little comforts beside them, I tell you, Mr. Shannon, those eyes looked up with their last dim life left in them as clear as the stars in the Southern Cross, Mr. Shannon. And now . . . now I am going to say something to you that will sound like something that only the spinster granddaughter of a minor romantic poet is likely to say. . . . Nothing I've ever seen has seemed as beautiful to me, not even the view from this verandah between the sky and the still-water beach, and lately . . . lately my grandfather's eyes have looked up at me like that. . . . [*She rises abruptly and crosses to the front of the verandah.*] Tell me, what is that sound I keep hearing down there?

SHANNON: There's a marimba band at the cantina on the beach.

HANNAH: I don't mean that, I mean that scraping, scuffling sound that I keep hearing under the verandah.

SHANNON: Oh, that. The Mexican boys that work here have caught an iguana and tied it up under the verandah, hitched it to a post, and naturally of course it's trying to scramble away. But it's got to the end of its rope, and get any further it cannot. Ha-ha—that's it. [*He quotes from* NONNO'S *poem:* "And still the orange," *etc.*] Do you have any life of your own—besides your water colors and sketches and your travels with Grampa?

HANNAH: We make a home for each other, my grandfather and I. Do you know what I mean by a home? I don't mean a regular home. I mean I don't mean what other people mean when they speak of a home, because I don't regard a home as a . . . well, as a place, a building . . . a house . . . of wood,

bricks, stone. I think of a home as being a thing that two people have between them in which each can . . . well, nest—
rest—live in, emotionally speaking. Does that make any sense
to you, Mr. Shannon?

SHANNON: Yeah, complete. But. . . .

HANNAH: Another incomplete sentence.

SHANNON: We better leave it that way. I might've said something to hurt you.

HANNAH: I'm not thin skinned, Mr. Shannon.

SHANNON: No, well, then, I'll say it. . . . [*He moves to the
liquor cart.*] When a bird builds a nest to rest in and live in, it
doesn't build it in a . . . a falling-down tree.

HANNAH: I'm not a bird, Mr. Shannon.

SHANNON: I was making an analogy, Miss Jelkes.

HANNAH: I thought you were making yourself another rum-
coco, Mr. Shannon.

SHANNON: Both. When a bird builds a nest, it builds it with
an eye for the . . . the relative permanence of the location,
and also for the purpose of mating and propagating its species.

HANNAH: I still say that I'm not a bird, Mr. Shannon, I'm a
human being and when a member of that fantastic species
builds a nest in the heart of another, the question of permanence isn't the first or even the last thing that's considered . . .
necessarily? . . . always? Nonno and I have been continually
reminded of the impermanence of things lately. We go back to
a hotel where we've been many times before and it isn't there
any more. It's been demolished and there's one of those glassy,
brassy new ones. Or if the old one's still there, the manager
or the Maitre D who always welcomed us back so cordially
before has been replaced by someone new who looks at us
with suspicion.

SHANNON: Yeah, but you still had each other.

HANNAH: Yes. We did.

SHANNON: But when the old gentleman goes?

HANNAH: Yes?

SHANNON: What will you do? Stop?

HANNAH: Stop or go on . . . probably go on.

SHANNON: Alone? Checking into hotels alone, eating alone at tables for one in a corner, the tables waiters call aces.

HANNAH: Thank you for your sympathy, Mr. Shannon, but in my profession I'm obliged to make quick contacts with strangers who turn to friends very quickly.

SHANNON: Customers aren't friends.

HANNAH: They turn to friends, if they're friendly.

SHANNON: Yeah, but how will it seem to be traveling alone after so many years of traveling with. . . .

HANNAH: I will know how it feels when I feel it—and don't say alone as if nobody had ever gone on alone. For instance, you.

SHANNON: I've always traveled with trainloads, planeloads and busloads of tourists.

HANNAH: That doesn't mean you're still not really alone.

SHANNON: I never fail to make an intimate connection with someone in my parties.

HANNAH: Yes, the youngest young lady, and I was on the verandah this afternoon when the latest of these young ladies gave a demonstration of how lonely the intimate connection has always been for you. The episode in the cold, inhuman hotel room, Mr. Shannon, for which you despise the lady almost as much as you despise yourself. Afterwards you are so polite to the lady that I'm sure it must chill her to the bone, the scrupulous little attentions that you pay her in return for your little enjoyment of her. The gentleman-of-Virginia act that you put on for her, your noblesse oblige treatment of her . . . Oh no, Mr. Shannon, don't kid yourself that you ever travel with someone. You have always traveled alone except for your spook, as you call it. He's your traveling companion. Nothing, nobody else has traveled with you.

SHANNON: Thank you for your sympathy, Miss Jelkes.

HANNAH: You're welcome, Mr. Shannon. And now I think I had better warm up the poppyseed tea for Nonno. Only a good night's sleep could make it possible for him to go on from here tomorrow.

SHANNON: Yes, well, if the conversation is over—I think I'll go down for a swim now.

HANNAH: To China?

SHANNON: No, not to China, just to the little island out here with the sleepy bar on it . . . called the Cantina Serena.

HANNAH: Why?

SHANNON: Because I'm not a nice drunk and I was about to ask you a not nice question.

HANNAH: Ask it. There's no set limit on questions here tonight.

SHANNON: And no set limit on answers?

HANNAH: None I can think of between you and me, Mr. Shannon.

SHANNON: That I will take you up on.

HANNAH: Do.

SHANNON: It's a bargain.

HANNAH: Only do lie back down in the hammock and drink a full cup of the poppyseed tea this time. It's warmer now and the sugared ginger will make it easier to get down.

SHANNON: All right. The question is this: have you never had in your life any kind of a lovelife? [HANNAH *stiffens for a moment*.] I thought you said there was no limit set on questions.

HANNAH: We'll make a bargain—I will answer your question *after* you've had a full cup of the poppyseed tea so you'll be able to get the good night's sleep you need, too. It's fairly warm now and the sugared ginger's made it much more— [*She sips the cup.*]—palatable.

SHANNON: You think I'm going to drift into dreamland so you can welch on the bargain? [*He accepts the cup from her.*]

HANNAH: I'm not a welcher on bargains. Drink it all. All. *All!*

SHANNON [*with a disgusted grimace as he drains the cup*]: *Great* Caesar's ghost. [*He tosses the cup off the verandah and falls into the hammock, chuckling.*] The oriental idea of a Mickey Finn, huh? Sit down where I can see you, Miss Jelkes honey. [*She sits down in a straight-back chair, some distance from the hammock.*] Where I can see you! I don't have an x-ray eye in the back of my head, Miss Jelkes. [*She moves the chair alongside the hammock.*] Further, further, up further. [*She complies.*] There now. Answer the question now, Miss Jelkes honey.

HANNAH: Would you mind repeating the question.

SHANNON [*slowly, with emphasis*]: Have you never had in all of your life and your travels any experience, any encounter, with what Larry-the-crackpot Shannon thinks of as a lovelife?

HANNAH: There are . . . worse things than chastity, Mr. Shannon.

SHANNON: Yeah, lunacy and death are both a little worse, *maybe!* But chastity isn't a thing that a beautiful woman or an attractive man falls into like a booby trap or an overgrown gopher hole, is it? [*There is a pause.*] I still think you are welching on the bargain and I. . . . [*He starts out of the hammock.*]

HANNAH: Mr. Shannon, this night is just as hard for me to get through as it is for you to get through. But it's you that are welching on the bargain, you're not staying in the hammock. Lie back down in the hammock. Now. Yes. Yes, I have had two experiences, well, encounters, with. . . .

SHANNON: *Two*, did you say?

HANNAH: Yes, I said two. And I wasn't exaggerating and don't you say "fantastic" before I've told you both stories. When I was sixteen, your favorite age, Mr. Shannon, each Saturday afternoon my grandfather Nonno would give me thirty cents, my allowance, my pay for my secretarial and housekeeping duties. Twenty-five cents for admission to the Saturday matinee at the Nantucket movie theatre and five cents extra for a bag of popcorn, Mr. Shannon. I'd sit at the almost empty back of the movie theatre so that the popcorn munching wouldn't disturb the other movie patrons. Well . . .

one afternoon a young man sat down beside me and pushed his . . . knee against mine and . . . I moved over two seats but he moved over beside me and continued this . . . pressure! I jumped up and screamed, Mr. Shannon. He was arrested for molesting a minor.

SHANNON: Is he still in the Nantucket jail?

HANNAH: No. I got him out. I told the police that it was a Clara Bow picture—it *was* a Clara Bow picture—and I was just overexcited.

SHANNON: Fantastic.

HANNAH: Yes, very! The second experience is much more recent, only two years ago, when Nonno and I were operating at the Raffles Hotel in Singapore, and doing very well there, making expenses and more. One evening in the Palm Court of the Raffles we met this middle-aged, sort of nondescript Australian salesman. You know—plump, bald-spotted, with a bad attempt at speaking with an upper-class accent and terribly overfriendly. He was alone and looked lonely. Grandfather said him a poem and I did a quick character sketch that was shamelessly flattering of him. He paid me more than my usual asking price and gave my grandfather five Malayan dollars, yes, and he even purchased one of my water colors. Then it was Nonno's bedtime. The Aussie salesman asked me out in a sampan with him. Well, he'd been so generous . . . I accepted. I did, I accepted. Grandfather went up to bed and I went out in the sampan with this ladies' underwear salesman. I noticed that he became more and more. . . .

SHANNON: What?

HANNAH: Well . . . *agitated* . . . as the afterglow of the sunset faded out on the water. [*She laughs with a delicate sadness.*] Well, finally, eventually, he leaned toward me . . . we were vis-à-vis in the sampan . . . and he looked intensely, passionately into my eyes. [*She laughs again.*] And he said to me: "Miss Jelkes? Will you do me a favor? Will you do something for me?" "What?" said I. "Well," said he, "if I turn my back, if I look the other way, will you take off some piece of your clothes and let me hold it, just hold it?"

SHANNON: Fantastic!

HANNAH: Then he said, "It will just take a few seconds." "Just a few seconds for what?" I asked him. [*She gives the same laugh again.*] He didn't say for what, but. . . .

SHANNON: His satisfaction?

HANNAH: Yes.

SHANNON: What did you do—in a situation like that?

HANNAH: I . . . gratified his request, I did! And he kept his promise. He did keep his back turned till I said ready and threw him . . . the part of my clothes.

SHANNON: What did he do with it?

HANNAH: He didn't move, except to seize the article he'd requested. I looked the other way while his satisfaction took place.

SHANNON: Watch out for commercial travelers in the Far East. Is that the moral, Miss Jelkes honey?

HANNAH: Oh, no, the moral is oriental. Accept whatever situation you cannot improve.

SHANNON: "When it's inevitable, lean back and enjoy it"—is that it?

HANNAH: He'd bought a water color. The incident was embarrassing, not violent. I left and returned unmolested. Oh, and the funniest part of all is that when we got back to the Raffles Hotel, he took the piece of apparel out of his pocket like a bashful boy producing an apple for his schoolteacher and tried to slip it into my hand in the elevator. I wouldn't accept it. I whispered, "Oh, please keep it, Mr. Willoughby!" He'd paid the asking price for my water color and somehow the little experience had been rather touching, I mean it was so *lonely*, out there in the sampan with violet streaks in the sky and this little middle-aged Australian making sounds like he was dying of asthma! And the planet Venus coming serenely out of a fair-weather cloud, over the Straits of Malacca. . . .

SHANNON: And that experience . . . you call that a. . . .

HANNAH: A love experience? Yes. I do call it one.

[*He regards her with incredulity, peering into her face so closely that she is embarrassed and becomes defensive.*]

SHANNON: That, that . . . sad, dirty little episode, you call it a . . . ?

HANNAH [*cutting in sharply*]: Sad it certainly was—for the odd little man—but why do you call it "dirty"?

SHANNON: How did you feel when you went into your bedroom?

HANNAH: Confused, I . . . a little confused, I suppose. . . . I'd known about loneliness—but not that degree or . . . depth of it.

SHANNON: You mean it didn't *disgust* you?

HANNAH: Nothing human disgusts me unless it's unkind, violent. And I told you how gentle he was—apologetic, shy, and really very, well, *delicate* about it. However, I do grant you it was on the rather fantastic level.

SHANNON: You're. . . .

HANNAH: I am *what?* "Fantastic?"

[*While they have been talking,* NONNO'S *voice has been heard now and then, mumbling, from his cubicle. Suddenly it becomes loud and clear.*]

NONNO:

And finally the broken stem,
The plummeting to earth and then. . . .

[*His voice subsides to its mumble.* SHANNON, *standing behind* HANNAH, *places his hand on her throat.*]

HANNAH: What is that for? Are you about to strangle me, Mr. Shannon?

SHANNON: You can't stand to be touched?

HANNAH: Save it for the widow. It isn't for me.

SHANNON: Yes, you're right. [*He removes his hand.*] I could do it with Mrs. Faulk, the inconsolable widow, but I couldn't with you.

HANNAH [*dryly and lightly*]: Spinster's loss, widow's gain, Mr. Shannon.

SHANNON: Or widow's loss, spinster's gain. Anyhow it sounds

like some old parlor game in a Virginia or Nantucket Island parlor. But . . . I wonder something. . . .

HANNAH: What do you wonder?

SHANNON: If we couldn't . . . *travel* together, I mean just *travel* together?

HANNAH: Could we? In your opinion?

SHANNON: Why not, I don't see why not.

HANNAH: I think the impracticality of the idea will appear much clearer to you in the morning, Mr. Shannon. [*She folds her dimly gold-lacquered fan and rises from her chair.*] Morning can always be counted on to bring us back to a more realistic level. . . . Good night, Mr. Shannon. I have to pack before I'm too tired to.

SHANNON: Don't leave me out here alone yet.

HANNAH: I have to pack now so I can get up at daybreak and try my luck in the plaza.

SHANNON: You won't sell a water color or sketch in that blazing hot plaza tomorrow. Miss Jelkes honey, I don't think you're operating on the realistic level.

HANNAH: Would I be if I thought we could travel together?

SHANNON: I still don't see why we couldn't.

HANNAH: Mr. Shannon, you're not well enough to travel anywhere with anybody right now. Does that sound cruel of me?

SHANNON: You mean that I'm stuck here for good? Winding up with the . . . inconsolable widow?

HANNAH: We all wind up with something or with someone, and if it's someone instead of just something, we're lucky, perhaps . . . unusually lucky. [*She starts to enter her cubicle, then turns to him again in the doorway.*] Oh, and tomorrow. . . . [*She touches her forehead as if a little confused as well as exhausted.*]

SHANNON: What about tomorrow?

HANNAH [*with difficulty*]: I think it might be better, tomorrow, if we avoid showing any particular interest in each other, because Mrs. Faulk is a morbidly jealous woman.

SHANNON: *Is* she?

HANNAH: Yes, she seems to have misunderstood our . . . sympathetic interest in each other. So I think we'd better avoid any more long talks on the verandah. I mean till she's thoroughly reassured it might be better if we just say good morning or good night to each other.

SHANNON: We don't even have to say that.

HANNAH: I will, but you don't have to answer.

SHANNON [*savagely*]: How about wall-tappings between us by way of communication? You know, like convicts in separate cells communicate with each other by tapping on the walls of the cells? One tap: I'm here. Two taps: are you there? Three taps: yes, I am. Four taps: that's good, we're together. *Christ!* . . . Here, take this. [*He snatches the gold cross from his pocket.*] Take my gold cross and hock it, it's 22-carat gold.

HANNAH: What do you, what are you . . . ?

SHANNON: There's a fine amethyst in it, it'll pay your travel expenses back to the States.

HANNAH: Mr. Shannon, you're making no sense at all now.

SHANNON: Neither are you, Miss Jelkes, talking about to-morrow, and. . . .

HANNAH: All I was saying was. . . .

SHANNON: You won't *be* here tomorrow! Had you forgotten you won't be here tomorrow?

HANNAH [*with a slight, shocked laugh*]: Yes, I *had*, I'd *forgotten!*

SHANNON: The widow wants you out and out you'll go, even if you sell your water colors like hotcakes to the pariah dogs in the plaza. [*He stares at her, shaking his head hopelessly.*]

HANNAH: I suppose you're right, Mr. Shannon. I must be too tired to think or I've contracted your fever. . . . It had actually slipped my mind for a moment that—

NONNO [*abruptly, from his cubicle*]: Hannah!

HANNAH [*rushing to his door*]: Yes, what is it, Nonno? [*He doesn't hear her and repeats her name louder.*] Here I am, I'm here.

NONNO: Don't come in yet, but stay where I can call you.

HANNAH: Yes, I'll *hear* you, Nonno. [*She turns toward SHANNON, drawing a deep breath.*]

SHANNON: Listen, if you don't take this gold cross that I never want on me again, I'm going to pitch it off the verandah at the spook in the rain forest. [*He raises an arm to throw it, but she catches his arm to restrain him.*]

HANNAH: All right, Mr. Shannon, I'll take it, I'll hold it for you.

SHANNON: Hock it, honey, you've got to.

HANNAH: Well, if I do, I'll mail the pawn ticket to you so you can redeem it, because you'll want it again, when you've gotten over your fever. [*She moves blindly down the verandah and starts to enter the wrong cubicle.*]

SHANNON: That isn't your cell, you went past it. [*His voice is gentle again.*]

HANNAH: I did, I'm sorry. I've never been this tired in all my life. [*She turns to face him again. He stares into her face. She looks blindly out, past him.*] Never! [*There is a slight pause.*] What did you say is making that constant, dry, scuffling sound beneath the verandah?

SHANNON: I told you.

HANNAH: I didn't hear you.

SHANNON: I'll get my flashlight, I'll show you. [*He lurches rapidly into his cubicle and back out with a flashlight.*] It's an iguana. I'll show you. . . . See? The iguana? At the end of its rope? Trying to go on past the end of its goddam rope? Like *you!* Like *me!* Like Grampa with his last poem!

[*In the pause which follows singing is heard from the beach.*]

HANNAH: What is a—what—iguana?

SHANNON: It's a kind of lizard—a big one, a giant one. The Mexican kids caught it and tied it up.

HANNAH: Why did they tie it up?

SHANNON: Because that's what they do. They tie them up and fatten them up and then eat them up, when they're ready for eating. They're a delicacy. Taste like white meat of chicken. At least the Mexicans think so. And also the kids, the Mexican kids, have a lot of fun with them, poking out their eyes with sticks and burning their tails with matches. You know? Fun? Like that?

HANNAH: Mr. Shannon, please go down and cut it loose!

SHANNON: I can't do that.

HANNAH: Why can't you?

SHANNON: Mrs. Faulk wants to eat it. I've got to please Mrs. Faulk, I am at her mercy. I am at her disposal.

HANNAH: I don't understand. I mean I don't understand how anyone could eat a big lizard.

SHANNON: Don't be so critical. If you got hungry enough you'd eat it too. You'd be surprised what people will eat if hungry. There's a lot of hungry people still in the world. Many have died of starvation, but a lot are still living and hungry, believe you me, if you will take my word for it. Why, when I was conducting a party of—*ladies?*—yes, ladies . . . through a country that shall be nameless but in this world, we were passing by rubberneck bus along a tropical coast when we saw a great mound of . . . well, the smell was unpleasant. One of my ladies said, "Oh, Larry, what is that?" My name being Lawrence, the most familiar ladies sometimes call me Larry. I didn't use the four-letter word for what the great mound was. I didn't think it was necessary to say it. Then she noticed, and I noticed too, a pair of very old natives of this nameless country, practically naked except for a few filthy rags, creeping and crawling about this mound of . . . and . . . occasionally stopping to pick something out of it, and pop it into their mouths. What? Bits of undigested . . . food particles, Miss Jelkes. [*There is silence for a moment. She makes a gagging sound in her throat and rushes the length of the verandah to the wooden steps and disappears for a while.* SHANNON *continues, to himself and the moon.*] Now why did I tell her that? Because it's true? That's no reason to tell her, because it's true.

Yeah. Because it's true was a good reason not to tell her. Except . . . I think I first *faced* it in that nameless country. The gradual, rapid, natural, unnatural—predestined, accidental—cracking up and going to pieces of young Mr. T. Lawrence Shannon, yes, still *young* Mr. T. Lawrence Shannon, by which rapid-slow process . . . his final tour of ladies through tropical countries. . . . Why did I say "tropical"? Hell! Yes! It's always been tropical countries I took ladies through. Does that, does that—huh?—signify something, I wonder? Maybe. Fast decay is a thing of hot climates, steamy, hot, wet climates, and I run back to them like a. . . . Incomplete sentence. . . . Always seducing a lady or two, or three or four or five ladies in the party, but really ravaging her first by pointing out to her the—what?—horrors? Yes, horrors!—of the tropical country being conducted a tour through. My . . . brain's going out now, like a failing—power. . . . So I stay here, I reckon, and live off la patrona for the rest of my life. Well, she's old enough to predecease me. She could check out of here first, and I imagine that after a couple of years of having to satisfy her I might be prepared for the shock of her passing on. . . . Cruelty . . . pity. What is it? . . . Don't know, all I know is. . . .

HANNAH [*from below the verandah*]: You're talking to yourself.

SHANNON: No. To you. I knew you could hear me out there, but not being able to see you I could say it easier, you know . . . ?

NONNO:
    A chronicle no longer gold,
    A bargaining with mist and mould. . . .

HANNAH [*coming back onto the verandah*]: I took a closer look at the iguana down there.

SHANNON: You did? How did you like it? Charming? Attractive?

HANNAH: No, it's not an attractive creature. Nevertheless I think it should be cut loose.

SHANNON: Iguanas have been known to bite their tails off when they're tied up by their tails.

HANNAH: This one is tied by its throat. It can't bite its own head off to escape from the end of the rope, Mr. Shannon. Can you look at me and tell me truthfully that you don't know it's able to feel pain and panic?

SHANNON: You mean it's one of God's creatures?

HANNAH: If you want to put it that way, yes, it is. Mr. Shannon, will you please cut it loose, set it free? Because if you don't, I will.

SHANNON: Can you look at *me* and tell *me* truthfully that this reptilian creature, tied up down there, doesn't mostly disturb you because of its parallel situation to your Grampa's dying-out effort to finish one last poem, Miss Jelkes?

HANNAH: Yes, I. . . .

SHANNON: Never mind completing that sentence. We'll play God tonight like kids play house with old broken crates and boxes. All right? Now Shannon is going to go down there with his machete and cut the damn lizard loose so it can run back to its bushes because God won't do it and we are going to play God here.

HANNAH: I knew you'd do that. And I thank you.

[SHANNON *goes down the two steps from the verandah with the machete. He crouches beside the cactus that hides the iguana and cuts the rope with a quick, hard stroke of the machete. He turns to look after its flight, as the low, excited mumble in cubicle 3 grows louder. Then* NONNO'S *voice turns to a sudden shout.*]

NONNO: *Hannah! Hannah!* [*She rushes to him, as he wheels himself out of his cubicle onto the verandah.*]

HANNAH: Grandfather! What is it?

NONNO: I! believe! it! is! *finished!* Quick, before I forget it— pencil, paper! Quick! please! Ready?

HANNAH: Yes. All ready, Grandfather.

NONNO [*in a loud, exalted voice*]:

How calmly does the orange branch
Observe the sky begin to blanch
Without a cry, without a prayer,
With no betrayal of despair.

Sometime while night obscures the tree
The zenith of its life will be
Gone past forever, and from thence
A second history will commence.

A chronicle no longer gold,
A bargaining with mist and mould,
And finally the broken stem
The plummeting to earth; and then

An intercourse not well designed
For beings of a golden kind
Whose native green must arch above
The earth's obscene, corrupting love.

And still the ripe fruit and the branch
Observe the sky begin to blanch
Without a cry, without a prayer,
With no betrayal of despair.

O Courage, could you not as well
Select a second place to dwell,
Not only in that golden tree
But in the frightened heart of me?

Have you got it?

HANNAH: Yes!

NONNO: All of it?

HANNAH: Every word of it.

NONNO: It is *finished?*

HANNAH: Yes.

NONNO: Oh! God! Finally finished?

HANNAH: Yes, finally finished. [*She is crying. The singing voices flow up from the beach.*]

NONNO: After waiting so long!

HANNAH: Yes, we waited so long.

NONNO: And it's good! It is *good?*

HANNAH: It's—it's. . . .

NONNO: What?

HANNAH: Beautiful, Grandfather! [*She springs up, a fist to her mouth.*] Oh, Grandfather, I am so happy for you. Thank you for writing such a lovely poem! It was worth the long wait. Can you sleep now, Grandfather?

NONNO: You'll have it typewritten tomorrow?

HANNAH: Yes. I'll have it typed up and send it off to *Harper's*.

NONNO: Hah? I didn't hear that, Hannah.

HANNAH [*shouting*]: I'll have it typed up tomorrow, and mail it to *Harper's* tomorrow! They've been waiting for it a long time, too! You know!

NONNO: Yes, I'd like to pray now.

HANNAH: Good night. Sleep now, Grandfather. You've finished your loveliest poem.

NONNO [*faintly, drifting off*]: Yes, thanks and praise . . .

[MAXINE *comes around the front of the verandah, followed by* PEDRO *playing a harmonica softly. She is prepared for a night swim, a vividly striped towel thrown over her shoulders. It is apparent that the night's progress has mellowed her spirit: her face wears a faint smile which is suggestive of those cool, impersonal, all-comprehending smiles on the carved heads of Egyptian or Oriental deities. Bearing a rum-coco, she approaches the hammock, discovers it empty, the ropes on the floor, and calls softly to* PEDRO.]

MAXINE: Shannon ha escapado! [PEDRO *goes on playing dreamily. She throws back her head and shouts.*] SHANNON! [*The call is echoed by the hill beyond.* PEDRO *advances a few steps and points under the verandah.*]

PEDRO: Miré. Allé 'hasta Shannon.

[SHANNON *comes into view from below the verandah, the severed rope and machete dangling from his hands.*]

MAXINE: What are you doing down there, Shannon?

SHANNON: I cut loose one of God's creatures at the end of the rope.

[HANNAH, *who has stood motionless with closed eyes behind*

the wicker chair, goes quietly toward the cubicles and out of the moon's glare.]

MAXINE [*tolerantly*]: What'd you do that for, Shannon.

SHANNON: So that one of God's creatures could scramble home safe and free. . . . A little act of grace, Maxine.

MAXINE [*smiling a bit more definitely*]: C'mon up here, Shannon. I want to talk to you.

SHANNON [*starting to climb onto the verandah, as* MAXINE *rattles the ice in the coconut shell*]: What d'ya want to talk about, Widow Faulk?

MAXINE: Let's go down and swim in that liquid moonlight.

SHANNON: Where did you pick up that poetic expression?

[MAXINE *glances back at* PEDRO *and dismisses him with,* "Vamos." *He leaves with a shrug, the harmonica fading out.*]

MAXINE: Shannon, I want you to stay with me.

SHANNON [*taking the rum-coco from her*]: You want a drinking companion?

MAXINE: No, I just want you to stay here, because I'm alone here now and I need somebody to help me manage the place.

[HANNAH *strikes a match for a cigarette.*]

SHANNON [*looking toward her*]: I want to remember that face. I won't see it again.

MAXINE: Let's go down to the beach.

SHANNON: I can make it down the hill, but not back up.

MAXINE: I'll get you back up the hill. [*They have started off now, toward the path down through the rain forest.*] I've got five more years, maybe ten, to make this place attractive to the male clientele, the middle-aged ones at least. And you can take care of the women that are with them. That's what you can do, you know that, Shannon.

[*He chuckles happily. They are now on the path,* MAXINE *half-leading, half-supporting him. Their voices fade as* HANNAH *goes into* NONNO'S *cubicle and comes back with a shawl, her cigarette left inside. She pauses between the door and the wicker chair and speaks to herself and the sky.*]

HANNAH: Oh, God, can't we stop now? Finally? Please let us. It's so quiet here, now.

[*She starts to put the shawl about* NONNO, *but at the same moment his head drops to the side. With a soft intake of breath, she extends a hand before his mouth to see if he is still breathing. He isn't. In a panicky moment, she looks right and left for someone to call to. There's no one. Then she bends to press her head to the crown of* NONNO'S *and the curtain starts to descend.*]

THE END

SIGNET Plays

☐ **THE AMERICAN DREAM and THE ZOO STORY by Edward Albee.** Two successful off-Broadway plays by the author of the hit, **Who's Afraid of Virginia Woolf?**
(#T4395—75¢)

☐ **THE SANDBOX and THE DEATH OF BESSIE SMITH by Edward Albee.** Two more off-Broadway hits by Albee: one about a scathing domestic tragedy, the other baring the ugly circumstances surrounding the death of a great Negro blues singer.
(#P2339—60¢)

☐ **LUTHER by John Osborne.** A brilliant play about the rebellious priest who challenged, and changed, the spiritual world of his time. By the author of **Look Back in Anger.**
(#Q3677—95¢)

☐ **A RAISIN IN THE SUN and THE SIGN IN SIDNEY BRUSTEIN'S WINDOW by Lorraine Hansberry.** Two outstanding plays: one, winner of the New York Drama Critics Award, about a young Negro father's struggle to break free from the barriers of prejudice, the other, portraying a modern-day intellectual's challenge of the negation and detachment of his fellow intellectuals. With a Foreword by John Braine and an introduction by Robert Nemiroff.
(#Q4111—95¢)
